CONTENTS

*   *   *   *   *

PART I

AT HOME

HIS WORSHIP THE GOOSEDRIVER

I

It was an amiable but deceitful afternoon in the third week of December. Snow fell heavily in the windows of confectioners' shops, and Father Christmas smiled in Keats's Bazaar the fawning smile of a myth who knows himself to be exploded; but beyond these and similar efforts to remedy the forgetfulness of a careless climate, there was no sign anywhere in the Five Towns, and especially in Bursley, of the immediate approach of the season of peace, goodwill, and gluttony on earth.

At the Tiger, next door to Keats's in the market-place, Mr. Josiah Topham Curtenty had put down his glass (the port was kept specially for him), and told his boon companion, Mr. Gordon, that he must be going. These two men had one powerful sentiment in common: they loved the same woman. Mr. Curtenty, aged twenty-six in heart, thirty-six in mind, and forty-six in looks, was fifty-six only in years. He was a rich man; he had made money as an earthenware manufacturer in the good old times before Satan was ingenious enough to invent German competition, American tariffs, and the price of coal; he was still making money with the aid of his son Harry, who now managed the works, but he never admitted that he was making it. No one has yet succeeded, and no one ever will succeed, in catching an earthenware manufacturer in the act of making money; he may confess with a sigh that he has performed the feat in the past, he may give utterance to a vague, preposterous hope that he will perform it again in the remote future, but as for surprising him in the very act, you would as easily surprise a hen laying an egg. Nowadays Mr. Curtenty, commercially secure, spent most of his energy in helping to shape and control the high destinies of the town. He was Deputy-Mayor, and Chairman of the General Purposes Committee of the Town Council; he was also a Guardian of the Poor, a Justice of the Peace, President of the Society for the Prosecution of Felons, a sidesman, an Oddfellow, and several other things that meant dining, shrewdness, and good-nature. He was a short, stiff, stout, red-faced man, jolly with the jollity that springs from a kind heart, a humorous disposition, a perfect digestion, and the respectful deference of one's bank-manager. Without being a member of the Browning Society, he held firmly to the belief that all's right with the world.

Mr. Gordon, who has but a sorry part in the drama, was a younger, quieter, less forceful person, rather shy; a municipal mediocrity, perhaps a little inflated that day by reason of his having been elected to the Chairmanship of the Gas and Lighting Committee.

Both men had sat on their committees at the Town Hall across the way that deceitful afternoon, and we see them now, after refreshment well earned and consumed, about to separate and sink into private life. But as they came out into

Tales of the Five Towns

by

Arnold Bennett

The Echo Library 2005

Published by

The Echo Library

Paperbackshop Ltd
Cockrup Farm House
Coln St Aldwyns
Cirencester GL7 5AZ

www.echo-library.com

ISBN 1-84637-660-2

the portico of the Tiger, the famous Calypso-like barmaid of the Tiger a hovering enchantment in the background, it occurred that a flock of geese were meditating, as geese will, in the middle of the road. The gooseherd, a shabby middle-aged man, looked as though he had recently lost the Battle of Marathon, and was asking himself whether the path of his retreat might not lie through the bar-parlour of the Tiger.

'Business pretty good?' Mr. Curtenty inquired of him cheerfully.

In the Five Towns business takes the place of weather as a topic of salutation.

'Business!' echoed the gooseherd.

In that one unassisted noun, scorning the aid of verb, adjective, or adverb, the gooseherd, by a masterpiece of profound and subtle emphasis, contrived to express the fact that he existed in a world of dead illusions, that he had become a convert to Schopenhauer, and that Mr. Curtenty's inapposite geniality was a final grievance to him.

'There ain't no business!' he added.

'Ah!' returned Mr. Curtenty, thoughtful: such an assertion of the entire absence of business was a reflection upon the town.

'Sithee!' said the gooseherd in ruthless accents, 'I druv these 'ere geese into this 'ere town this morning.' (Here he exaggerated the number of miles traversed.) 'Twelve geese and two gander—a Brent and a Barnacle. And how many is there now? How many?'

'Fourteen,' said Mr. Gordon, having counted; and Mr. Curtenty gazed at him in reproach, for that he, a Town Councillor, had thus mathematically demonstrated the commercial decadence of Bursley.

'Market overstocked, eh?' Mr. Curtenty suggested, throwing a side-glance at Callear the poulterer's close by, which was crammed with everything that flew, swam, or waddled.

'Call this a market?' said the gooseherd. 'T'st tak' my lot over to Hanbridge, wheer there *is* a bit doing, by all accounts.'

Now, Mr. Curtenty had not the least intention of buying those geese, but nothing could be better calculated to straighten the back of a Bursley man than a reference to the mercantile activity of Hanbridge, that Chicago of the Five Towns.

'How much for the lot?' he inquired.

In that moment he reflected upon his reputation; he knew that he was a cure, a card, a character; he knew that everyone would think it just like Jos Curtenty, the renowned Deputy-Mayor of Bursley, to stand on the steps of the Tiger and pretend to chaffer with a gooseherd for a flock of geese. His imagination caught the sound of an oft-repeated inquiry, 'Did ye hear about old Jos's latest—trying to buy them there geese?' and the appreciative laughter that would follow.

The gooseherd faced him in silence.

'Well,' said Mr. Curtenty again, his eyes twinkling, 'how much for the lot?'

The gooseherd gloomily and suspiciously named a sum.

Mr. Curtenty named a sum startlingly less, ending in sixpence.

'I'll tak' it,' said the gooseherd, in a tone that closed on the bargain like a vice.

The Deputy-Mayor perceived himself the owner of twelve geese and two ganders—one Brent, one Barnacle. It was a shock, but he sustained it. Involuntarily he looked at Mr. Gordon.

'How are you going to get 'em home, Curtenty?' asked Gordon, with coarse sarcasm; 'drive 'em?'

Nettled, Mr. Curtenty retorted:

'Now, then, Gas Gordon!'

The barmaid laughed aloud at this sobriquet, which that same evening was all over the town, and which has stuck ever since to the Chairman of the Gas and Lighting Committee. Mr. Gordon wished, and has never ceased to wish, either that he had been elected to some other committee, or that his name had begun with some other letter.

The gooseherd received the purchase-money like an affront, but when Mr. Curtenty, full of private mirth, said, 'Chuck us your stick in,' he give him the stick, and smiled under reservation. Jos Curtenty had no use for the geese; he could conceive no purpose which they might be made to serve, no smallest corner for them in his universe. Nevertheless, since he had rashly stumbled into a ditch, he determined to emerge from it grandly, impressively, magnificently. He instantaneously formed a plan by which he would snatch victory out of defeat. He would take Gordon's suggestion, and himself drive the geese up to his residence in Hillport, that lofty and aristocratic suburb. It would be an immense, an unparalleled farce; a wonder, a topic for years, the crown of his reputation as a card.

He announced his intention with that misleading sobriety and ordinariness of tone which it has been the foible of many great humorists to assume. Mr. Gordon lifted his head several times very quickly, as if to say, 'What next?' and then actually departed, which was a clear proof that the man had no imagination and no soul.

The gooseherd winked.

'You be rightly called "Curtenty," mester,' said he, and passed into the Tiger.

'That's the best joke I ever heard,' Jos said to himself 'I wonder whether he saw it.'

Then the procession of the geese and the Deputy-Mayor commenced. Now, it is not to be assumed that Mr. Curtenty was necessarily bound to look foolish in the driving of geese. He was no nincompoop. On the contrary, he was one of those men who, bringing common-sense and presence of mind to every action of their lives, do nothing badly, and always escape the ridiculous. He marshalled his geese with notable gumption, adopted towards them exactly the correct stress of persuasion, and presently he smiled to see them preceding him in the direction of Hillport. He looked neither to right nor left, but simply at his geese, and thus the quidnuncs of the market-place and the supporters of shop-fronts were unable to catch his eye. He tried to feel like a gooseherd; and such was his histrionic quality, his instinct for the dramatic, he *was* a gooseherd, despite his blue Melton overcoat, his hard felt hat with the flattened top, and that opulent-curving collar which was the secret despair of the young dandies of Hillport. He had the most natural air in the world. The geese were the victims of this imaginative effort of Mr. Curtenty's. They took him seriously as a gooseherd. These fourteen intelligences, each with an object in life, each bent on self-aggrandisement and the satisfaction of desires, began to follow the line of least resistance in regard to the superior intelligence unseen but felt behind them, feigning, as geese will, that it suited them so to submit, and that in reality they were still quite independent. But in the peculiar eye of the Barnacle gander, who was leading, an observer with sufficient fancy might have deciphered a mild revolt against this triumph of the absurd, the accidental, and the futile; a passive yet Promethean spiritual defiance of the supreme powers.

Mr. Curtenty got his fourteen intelligences safely across the top of St. Luke's Square, and gently urged them into the steep defile of Oldcastle Street. By this time rumour had passed in front of him and run off down side-streets like water let into an irrigation system. At every corner was a knot of people, at most windows a face. And the Deputy-Mayor never spoke nor smiled. The farce was enormous; the memory of it would survive revolutions and religions.

Halfway down Oldcastle Street the first disaster happened. Electric tramways had not then knitted the Five Towns in a network of steel; but the last word of civilization and refinement was about to be uttered, and a gang of men were making patterns with wires on the skyscape of Oldcastle Street. One of the wires, slipping from its temporary gripper, swirled with an extraordinary sound into the roadway, and writhed there in spirals. Several of Mr. Curtenty's geese were knocked down, and rose obviously annoyed; but the Barnacle gander fell with a clinging circle of wire round his muscular, glossy neck, and did not rise again. It was a violent, mysterious, agonizing, and sudden death for him, and must have confirmed his theories about the arbitrariness of things. The thirteen passed pitilessly on. Mr. Curtenty freed the gander from the coiling wire, and picked it up, but, finding it far too heavy to carry, he handed it to a Corporation road-sweeper.

'I'll send for it,' he said; 'wait here.'

These were the only words uttered by him during a memorable journey.

The second disaster was that the deceitful afternoon turned to rain—cold, cruel rain, persistent rain, full of sinister significance. Mr. Curtenty ruefully raised the velvet of his Melton. As he did so a brougham rolled into Oldcastle Street, a little in front of him, from the direction of St. Peter's Church, and vanished towards Hillport. He knew the carriage; he had bought it and paid for it. Deep, far down, in his mind stirred the thought:

'I'm just the least bit glad she didn't see me.'

He had the suspicion, which recurs even to optimists, that happiness is after all a chimera.

The third disaster was that the sun set and darkness descended. Mr. Curtenty had, unfortunately, not reckoned with this diurnal phenomenon; he had not thought upon the undesirability of being under compulsion to drive geese by the sole illumination of gas-lamps lighted by Corporation gas.

After this disasters multiplied. Dark and the rain had transformed the farce into something else. It was five-thirty when at last he reached The Firs, and the garden of The Firs was filled with lamentable complainings of a remnant of geese. His man Pond met him with a stable-lantern.

'Damp, sir,' said Pond.

'Oh, nowt to speak of,' said Mr. Curtenty, and, taking off his hat, he shot the fluid contents of the brim into Pond's face. It was his way of dotting the 'i' of irony. 'Missis come in?'

'Yes, sir; I have but just rubbed the horse down.'

So far no reference to the surrounding geese, all forlorn in the heavy winter rain.

'I've gotten a two-three geese and one gander here for Christmas,' said Mr. Curtenty after a pause. To inferiors he always used the dialect.

'Yes, sir.'

'Turn 'em into th' orchard, as you call it.'

'Yes, sir.'

'They aren't all here. Thou mun put th' horse in the trap and fetch the rest thysen.'

'Yes, sir.'

'One's dead. A roadman's takkin' care on it in Oldcastle Street. He'll wait for thee. Give him sixpence.'

'Yes, sir.'

'There's another got into th' cut [canal].'

'Yes, sir.'

'There's another strayed on the railway-line—happen it's run over by this.'

'Yes, sir.'

'And one's making the best of her way to Oldcastle. I couldna coax her in here.'

'Yes, sir.'

'Collect 'em.'

'Yes, sir.'

Mr. Curtenty walked away towards the house.

'Mester!' Pond called after him, flashing the lantern.

'Well, lad?'

'There's no gander i' this lot.'

'Hast forgotten to count thysen?' Mr. Curtenty answered blithely from the shelter of the side-door.

But within himself he was a little crest-fallen to think that the surviving gander should have escaped his vigilance, even in the darkness. He had set out to drive the geese home, and he had driven them home, most of them. He had kept his temper, his dignity, his cheerfulness. He had got a bargain in geese. So much was indisputable ground for satisfaction. And yet the feeling of an anticlimax would not be dismissed. Upon the whole, his transit lacked glory. It had begun in splendour, but it had ended in discomfort and almost ignominy. Nevertheless, Mr. Curtenty's unconquerable soul asserted itself in a quite genuine and tuneful whistle as he entered the house.

The fate of the Brent gander was never ascertained.

II

The dining-room of The Firs was a spacious and inviting refectory, which owed nothing of its charm to William Morris, Regent Street, or the Arts and Crafts Society. Its triple aim, was richness, solidity, and comfort, but especially comfort; and this aim was achieved in new oak furniture of immovable firmness, in a Turkey carpet which swallowed up the feet like a feather bed, and in large oil-paintings, whose darkly-glinting frames were a guarantee of their excellence. On a winter's night, as now, the room was at its richest, solidest, most comfortable. The blue plush curtains were drawn on their stout brass rods across door and French window. Finest selected silkstone fizzed and flamed in a patent grate which had the extraordinary gift of radiating heat into the apartment instead of up the chimney. The shaded Welsbach lights of the chandelier cast a dazzling luminance on the tea-table of snow and silver, while leaving the pictures in a gloom so discreet that not Ruskin himself could have decided whether these were by Whistler or Peter Paul Rubens. On either side of the marble mantelpiece were two easy-chairs of an immense, incredible capacity, chairs of crimson plush for Titans, chairs softer than moss, more pliant than a loving heart, more enveloping than a caress. In one of these chairs, that to the left of the fireplace, Mr. Curtenty was accustomed to snore every Saturday and Sunday afternoon, and almost every evening. The other was usually empty, but to-night it was occupied by Mrs. Curtenty, the jewel of the casket. In the presence of her husband she always used a small rocking-chair of ebonized cane.

To glance at this short, slight, yet plump little creature as she reclined crosswise in the vast chair, leaving great spaces of the seat unfilled, was to think rapturously to one's self: *This is a woman*. Her fluffy head was such a dot against the back of the chair, the curve of her chubby ringed hand above the head was so adorable, her black eyes were so provocative, her slippered feet so wee—yes, and there was something so mysteriously thrilling about the fall of her skirt that you knew instantly her name was Clara, her temper both fiery and obstinate, and her personality distracting. You knew that she was one of those women of frail physique who can endure fatigues that would destroy a camel; one of those dæmonic women capable of doing without sleep for ten nights in order to nurse you; capable of dying and seeing you die rather than give way about the tint of a necktie; capable of laughter and tears simultaneously; capable of never being in the wrong except for the idle whim of so being. She had a big mouth and very wide nostrils, and her years were thirty-five. It was no matter; it would have been no matter had she been a hundred and thirty-five. In short....

Clara Curtenty wore tight-fitting black silk, with a long gold chain that descended from her neck nearly to her waist, and was looped up in the middle to an old-fashioned gold brooch. She was in mourning for a distant relative. Black pre-eminently suited her. Consequently her distant relatives died at frequent intervals.

The basalt clock on the mantelpiece trembled and burst into the song of six. Clara Curtenty rose swiftly from the easy-chair, and took her seat in front of the tea-tray. Almost at the same moment a neat black-and-white parlourmaid brought in teapot, copper kettle, and a silver-covered dish containing hot pikelets; then departed. Clara was alone again; not the same Clara now, but a personage demure, prim, precise, frightfully upright of back—a sort of impregnable stronghold—without doubt a Deputy-Mayoress.

At five past six Josiah Curtenty entered the room, radiant from a hot bath, and happy in dry clothes—a fine, if mature, figure of a man. His presence filled the whole room.

'Well, my chuck!' he said, and kissed her on the cheek.

She gazed at him with a look that might mean anything. Did she raise her cheek to his greeting, or was it fancy that she had endured, rather than accepted, his kiss? He was scarcely sure. And if she had endured instead of accepting the kiss, was her mood to be attributed to his lateness for tea, or to the fact that she was aware of the episode of the geese? He could not divine.

'Pikelets! Good!' he exclaimed, taking the cover off the dish.

This strong, successful, and dominant man adored his wife, and went in fear of her. She was his first love, but his second spouse. They had been married ten years. In those ten years they had quarrelled only five times, and she had changed the very colour of his life. Till his second marriage he had boasted that he belonged to the people and retained the habits of the people. Clara, though she also belonged to the people, very soon altered all that. Clara had a passion for the genteel. Like many warm-hearted, honest, clever, and otherwise sensible persons, Clara was a snob, but a charming little snob. She ordered him to forget that he belonged to the people. She refused to listen when he talked in the dialect. She made him dress with opulence, and even with tidiness; she made him buy a fashionable house and fill it with fine furniture; she made him buy a brougham in which her gentility could pay calls and do shopping (she shopped in Oldcastle, where a decrepit aristocracy of tradesmen sneered at Hanbridge's lack of style); she had her 'day'; she taught the servants to enter the reception-rooms without knocking; she took tea in bed in the morning, and tea in the afternoon in the drawing-room. She would have instituted dinner at seven, but she was a wise woman, and realized that too much tyranny often means revolution and the crumbling of-thrones; therefore the ancient plebeian custom of high tea at six was allowed to persist and continue.

She it was who had compelled Josiah (or bewitched, beguiled, coaxed and wheedled him), after a public refusal, to accept the unusual post of Deputy-Mayor. In two years' time he might count on being Mayor. Why, then, should Clara have been so anxious for this secondary dignity? Because, in that year of royal festival, Bursley, in common with many other boroughs, had had a fancy to choose a Mayor out of the House of Lords. The Earl of Chell, a magnate of the county, had consented to wear the mayoral chain and dispense the mayoral hospitalities on condition that he was provided with a deputy for daily use.

It was the idea of herself being deputy to the lovely, meddlesome, and arrogant Countess of Chell that had appealed to Clara.

The deputy of a Countess at length spoke.

'Will Harry be late at the works again to-night?' she asked in her colder, small-talk manner, which committed her to nothing, as Josiah well knew.

Her way of saying that word 'Harry' was inimitably significant. She gave it an air. She liked Harry, and she liked Harry's name, because it had a Kensingtonian sound. Harry, so accomplished in business, was also a dandy, and he was a dog. 'My stepson'—she loved to introduce him, so tall, manly, distinguished, and dandiacal. Harry, enriched by his own mother, belonged to a London club; he ran down to Llandudno for week-ends; and it was reported that he had been behind the scenes at the Alhambra. Clara felt for the word 'Harry' the unreasoning affection which most women lavish on 'George.'

'Like as not,' said Josiah. 'I haven't been to the works this afternoon.'

Another silence fell, and then Josiah, feeling himself unable to bear any further suspense as to his wife's real mood and temper, suddenly determined to tell her all about the geese, and know the worst. And precisely at the instant that he opened his mouth, the maid opened the door and announced:

'Mr. Duncalf wishes to see you at once, sir. He won't keep you a minute.'

'Ask him in here, Mary,' said the Deputy-Mayoress sweetly; 'and bring another cup and saucer.'

Mr. Duncalf was the Town Clerk of Bursley: legal, portly, dry, and a little shy.

'I won't stop, Curtenty. How d'ye do, Mrs. Curtenty? No, thanks, really——' But she, smiling, exquisitely gracious, flattered and smoothed him into a chair.

'Any interesting news, Mr. Duncalf?' she said, and added: 'But we're glad that *anything* should have brought you in.'

'Well,' said Duncalf, 'I've just had a letter by the afternoon post from Lord Chell.'

'Oh, the Earl! Indeed; how very interesting.'

'What's he after?' inquired Josiah cautiously.

'He says he's just been appointed Governor of East Australia—announcement 'll be in to-morrow's papers—and so he must regretfully resign the mayoralty. Says he'll pay the fine, but of course we shall have to remit that by special resolution of the Council.'

'Well, I'm damned!' Josiah exclaimed.

'Topham!' Mrs. Curtenty remonstrated, but with a delightful acquitting dimple. She never would call him Josiah, much less Jos. Topham came more easily to her lips, and sometimes Top.

'Your husband,' said Mr. Duncalf impressively to Clara, 'will, of course, have to step into the Mayor's shoes, and you'll have to fill the place of the Countess.' He paused, and added: 'And very well you'll do it, too—very well. Nobody better.'

The Town Clerk frankly admired Clara.

'Mr. Duncalf—Mr. Duncalf!' She raised a finger at him. 'You are the most shameless flatterer in the town.'

The flatterer was flattered. Having delivered the weighty news, he had leisure to savour his own importance as the bearer of it. He drank a cup of tea. Josiah was thoughtful, but Clara brimmed over with a fascinating loquacity. Then Mr. Duncalf said that he must really be going, and, having arranged with the Mayor-elect to call a special meeting of the Council at once, he did go, all the while wishing he had the enterprise to stay.

Josiah accompanied him to the front-door. The sky had now cleared.

'Thank ye for calling,' said the host.

'Oh, that's all right. Good-night, Curtenty. Got that goose out of the canal?'

So the story was all abroad!

Josiah returned to the dining-room, imperceptibly smiling. At the door the sight of his wife halted him. The face of that precious and adorable woman flamed out lightning and all menace and offence. Her louring eyes showed what a triumph of dissimulation she must have achieved in the presence of Mr. Duncalf, but now she could speak her mind.

'Yes, Topham!' she exploded, as though finishing an harangue. 'And on this day of all days you choose to drive geese in the public road behind my carriage!'

Jos was stupefied, annihilated.

'Did you see me, then, Clarry?'

He vainly tried to carry it off.

'Did I see you? Of course I saw you!'

She withered him up with the hot wind of scorn.

'Well,' he said foolishly, 'how was I to know that the Earl would resign just to-day?'

'How were you to——?'

Harry came in for his tea. He glanced from one to the other, discreet, silent. On the way home he had heard the tale of the geese in seven different forms. The Deputy-Mayor, so soon to be Mayor, walked out of the room.

'Pond has just come back, father,' said Harry; 'I drove up the hill with him.'

And as Josiah hesitated a moment in the hall, he heard Clara exclaim, 'Oh, Harry!'

'Damn!' he murmured.

III

The *Signal* of the following day contained the announcement which Mr. Duncalf had forecast; it also stated, on authority, that Mr. Josiah Curtenty would wear the mayoral chain of Bursley immediately, and added as its own private opinion that, in default of the Right Honourable the Earl of Chell and his Countess, no better 'civic heads' could have been found than Mr. Curtenty and his charming wife. So far the tone of the *Signal* was unimpeachable. But underneath all this was a sub-title, 'Amusing Exploit of the Mayor-elect,' followed by an amusing description of the procession of the geese, a description which concluded by referring to Mr. Curtenty as His Worship the Goosedriver.

Hanbridge, Knype, Longshaw, and Turnhill laughed heartily, and perhaps a little viciously, at this paragraph, but Bursley was annoyed by it. In print the affair did not look at all well. Bursley prided itself on possessing a unique dignity as the 'Mother of the Five Towns,' and to be presided over by a goosedriver, however humorous and hospitable he might be, did not consort with that dignity. A certain Mayor of Longshaw, years before, had driven a sow to market, and derived a tremendous advertisement therefrom, but Bursley had no wish to rival Longshaw in any particular. Bursley regarded Longshaw as the Inferno of the Five Towns. In Bursley you were bidden to go to Longshaw as you were bidden to go to ... Certain acute people in Hillport saw nothing but a paralyzing insult in the opinion of the *Signal* (first and foremost a Hanbridge organ), that Bursley could find no better civic head than Josiah Curtenty. At least three Aldermen and seven Councillors privately, and in the Tiger, disagreed with any such view of Bursley's capacity to find heads.

And underneath all this brooding dissatisfaction lurked the thought, as the alligator lurks in a muddy river, that 'the Earl wouldn't like it'—meaning the geese episode. It was generally felt that the Earl had been badly treated by Jos Curtenty. The town could not explain its sentiments—could not argue about them. They were not, in fact, capable of logical justification; but they were there, they violently existed. It would have been useless to point out that if the inimitable Jos had not been called to the mayoralty the episode of the geese would have passed as a gorgeous joke; that everyone had been vastly amused by it until that desolating issue of the *Signal* announced the Earl's retirement; that Jos Curtenty could not possibly have foreseen what was about to happen; and that, anyhow, goosedriving was less a crime than a social solecism, and less a social solecism than a brilliant eccentricity. Bursley was hurt, and logic is no balm for wounds.

Some may ask: If Bursley was offended, why did it not mark its sense of Josiah's failure to read the future by electing another Mayor? The answer is, that while all were agreed that his antic was inexcusable, all were equally agreed to pretend that it was a mere trifle of no importance; you cannot deprive a man of his prescriptive right for a mere trifle of no importance. Besides, nobody could be so foolish as to imagine that goosedriving, though reprehensible in a Mayor about to succeed an Earl, is an act of which official notice can be taken.

The most curious thing in the whole imbroglio is that Josiah Curtenty secretly agreed with his wife and the town. He was ashamed, overset. His procession of geese appeared to him in an entirely new light, and he had the strength of mind to admit to himself, 'I've made a fool of myself.'

Harry went to London for a week, and Josiah, under plea of his son's absence, spent eight hours a day at the works. The brougham remained in the coach-house.

The Town Council duly met in special conclave, and Josiah Topham Curtenty became Mayor of Bursley.

Shortly after Christmas it was announced that the Mayor and Mayoress had decided to give a New Year's treat to four hundred poor old people in the St. Luke's covered market. It was also spread about that this treat would eclipse and extinguish all previous treats of a similar nature, and that it might be accepted as some slight foretaste of the hospitality which the Mayor and Mayoress would dispense in that memorable year of royal festival. The treat was to occur on January 9, the Mayoress's birthday.

On January 7 Josiah happened to go home early. He was proceeding into the drawing-room without enthusiasm to greet his wife, when he heard voices within; and one voice was the voice of Gas Gordon.

Jos stood still. It has been mentioned that Gordon and the Mayor were in love with the same woman. The Mayor had easily captured her under the very guns of his not formidable rival, and he had always thereafter felt a kind of benevolent, good-humoured, contemptuous pity for Gordon—Gordon, whose life was a tragic blank; Gordon, who lived, a melancholy and defeated bachelor, with his mother and two unmarried sisters older than himself. That Gordon still worshipped at the shrine did not disturb him; on the contrary, it pleased him. Poor Gordon!

'But, really, Mrs. Curtenty,' Gordon was saying—'really, you know I—that—is—really—'

'To please me!' Mrs. Curtenty entreated, with a seductive charm that Jos felt even outside the door.

Then there was a pause.

'Very well,' said Gordon.

Mr. Curtenty tiptoed away and back into the street. He walked in the dark nearly to Oldcastle, and returned about six o'clock. But Clara said no word of Gordon's visit. She had scarcely spoken to Topham for three weeks.

The next morning, as Harry was departing to the works, Mrs. Curtenty followed the handsome youth into the hall.

'Harry,' she whispered, 'bring me two ten-pound notes this afternoon, will you, and say nothing to your father.'

IV

Gas Gordon was to be on the platform at the poor people's treat. As he walked down Trafalgar Road his eye caught a still-exposed fragment of a decayed bill on a hoarding. It referred to a meeting of the local branch of the Anti-Gambling League a year ago in the lecture-hall of the Wesleyan Chapel, and it said that Councillor Gordon would occupy the chair on that occasion. Mechanically Councillor Gordon stopped and tore the fragment away from the hoarding.

The treat, which took the form of a dinner, was an unqualified success; it surpassed all expectations. Even the diners themselves were satisfied—a rare thing at such affairs. Goose was a prominent item in the menu. After the repast the replete guests were entertained from the platform, the Mayor being, of course, in the chair. Harry sang 'In Old Madrid,' accompanied by his stepmother, with faultless expression. Mr. Duncalf astonished everybody with the famous North-Country recitation, 'The Patent Hair-brushing Mashane.' There were also a banjo solo, a skirt dance of discretion, and a campanological turn. At last, towards ten o'clock, Mr. Gordon, who had hitherto done nothing, rose in his place, amid good-natured cries of 'Gas!'

'I feel sure you will all agree with me,' he began, 'that this evening would not be complete without a vote of thanks—a very hearty vote of thanks—to our excellent host and chairman.'

Ear-splitting applause.

'I've got a little story to tell you,' he continued—'a story that up to this moment has been a close secret between his Worship the Mayor and myself.' His Worship looked up sharply at the speaker. 'You've heard about some geese, I reckon. (*Laughter.*) Well, you've not heard all, but I'm going to tell you. I can't keep it to myself any longer. You think his Worship drove those geese—I hope they're digesting well (*loud laughter*)—just for fun. He didn't. I was with him when he bought them, and I happened to say that goosedriving was a very difficult accomplishment.'

'Depends on the geese!' shouted a voice.

'Yes, it does,' Mr. Gordon admitted. 'Well, his Worship contradicted me, and we had a bit of an argument. I don't bet, as you know—at least, not often—but I don't mind confessing that I offered to bet him a sovereign he couldn't drive his geese half a mile. "Look here, Gordon," he said to me: "there's a lot of distress in the town just now—trade bad, and so on, and so on. I'll lay you a level ten pounds I drive these geese to Hillport myself, the loser to give the money to charity." "Done," I said. "Don't say anything about it," he says. "I won't," I says— but I am doing. (*Applause.*) I feel it my duty to say something about it. (*More applause.*) Well, I lost, as you all know. He drove 'em to Hillport. ('*Good old Jos!*') That's not all. The Mayor insisted on putting his own ten pounds to mine and making it twenty. Here are the two identical notes, his and mine.' Mr. Gordon waved the identical notes amid an uproar. 'We've decided that everyone who has dined here to-night shall receive a brand-new shilling. I see Mr. Septimus Lovatt from the bank there with a bag. He will attend to you as you go out. (*Wild outbreak and tumult of rapturous applause.*) And now three cheers for your Mayor—and Mayoress!'

It was colossal, the enthusiasm.

'*And* for Gas Gordon!' called several voices.

The cheers rose again in surging waves.

Everyone remarked that the Mayor, usually so imperturbable, was quite overcome—seemed as if he didn't know where to look.

Afterwards, as the occupants of the platform descended, Mr. Gordon glanced into the eyes of Mrs. Curtenty, and found there his exceeding reward. The mediocrity had blossomed out that evening into something new and strange. Liar, deliberate liar and self-accused gambler as he was, he felt that he had lived during that speech; he felt that it was the supreme moment of his life.

'What a perfectly wonderful man your husband is!' said Mrs. Duncalf to Mrs. Curtenty.

Clara turned to her husband with a sublime gesture of satisfaction. In the brougham, going home, she bewitched him with wifely endearments. She could afford to do so. The stigma of the geese episode was erased.

But the barmaid of the Tiger, as she let down her bright hair that night in the attic of the Tiger, said to herself, 'Well, of all the——' Just that.

THE ELIXIR OF YOUTH

It was Monday afternoon of Bursley Wakes—not our modern rectified festival, but the wild and naïve orgy of seventy years ago, the days of bear-baiting and of bull-baiting, from which latter phrase, they say, the town derives its name. In those times there was a town-bull, a sort of civic beast; and a certain notorious character kept a bear in his pantry. The 'beating' (baiting) occurred usually on Sunday mornings at six o'clock, with formidable hungry dogs; and little boys used to look forward eagerly to the day when they would be old enough to be permitted to attend. On Sunday afternoons colliers and potters, gathered round the jawbone of a whale which then stood as a natural curiosity on the waste space near the corn-mill, would discuss the fray, and make bets for next Sunday, while the exhausted dogs licked their wounds, or died. During the Wakes week bull and bear were baited at frequent intervals, according to popular demand, for thousands of sportsmen from neighbouring villages seized the opportunity of the fair to witness the fine beatings for which Bursley was famous throughout the country of the Five Towns. In that week the Wakes took possession of the town, which yielded itself with savage abandonment to all the frenzies of license. The public-houses remained continuously open night and day, and the barmen and barmaids never went to bed; every inn engaged special 'talent' in order to attract custom, and for a hundred hours the whole thronged town drank, drank, until the supply of coin of George IV., converging gradually into the coffers of a few persons, ceased to circulate. Towards the end of the Wakes, by way of a last ecstasy, the cockfighters would carry their birds, which had already fought and been called off, perhaps, half a dozen times, to the town-field (where the discreet 40 per cent. brewery now stands), and there match them to a finish. It was a spacious age.

On this Monday afternoon in June the less fervid activities of the Wakes were proceeding as usual in the market-place, overshadowed by the Town Hall—not the present stone structure with its gold angel, but a brick edifice built on an ashlar basement. Hobby-horses and revolving swing-boats, propelled, with admirable economy to the proprietors, by privileged boys who took their pay in an occasional ride, competed successfully with the skeleton man, the fat or bearded woman, and Aunt Sally. The long toy-tents, artfully roofed with a tinted cloth which permitted only a soft, mellow light to illuminate the wares displayed, were crowded with jostling youth and full of the sound of whistles, 'squarkers,' and various pipes; and multitudes surrounded the gingerbread, nut, and savoury stalls which lined both sides of the roadway as far as Duck Bank. In front of the numerous boxing-booths experts of the 'fancy,' obviously out of condition, offered to fight all comers, and were not seldom well thrashed by impetuous champions of local fame. There were no photographic studios and no cocoanut-shies, for these things had not been thought of; and to us moderns the fair, despite its uncontrolled exuberance of revelry, would have seemed strangely quiet, since neither steam-organ nor hooter nor hurdy-gurdy was there to overwhelm the ear with crashing waves of gigantic sound. But if the special phenomena of a later day were missing from the carnival, others, as astonishing to us as the steam-organ would have been to those uncouth roisterers, were certainly present. Chief, perhaps, among these was the man who retailed the elixir of youth, the veritable *eau de jouvence*, to credulous drinkers at sixpence a bottle. This magician, whose dark mysterious face and glittering eyes indicated a strain of Romany blood, and whose accent proved that he had at any rate lived much in Yorkshire, had a small booth opposite the watch-house under the Town Hall. On a banner suspended in front of it was painted the legend:

**THE INCA OF PERU'S
ELIXER OF YOUTH
SOLD HERE.
ETERNAL YOUTH FOR ALL.
DRINK THIS AND YOU WILL NEVER GROW OLD
AS SUPPLIED TO THE NOBILITY & GENTRY
SIXPENCE PER BOT.
WALK IN, WALK IN, &
CONSULT THE INCA OF PERU.**

The Inca of Peru, dressed in black velveteens, with a brilliant scarf round his neck, stood at the door of his tent, holding an empty glass in one jewelled hand, and with the other twirling a long and silken moustache. Handsome, graceful, and thoroughly inured to the public gaze, he fronted a small circle of gapers like an actor adroit to make the best of himself, and his tongue wagged fast enough to wag a man's leg off. At a casual glance he might have been taken for thirty, but his age was fifty and more—if you could catch him in the morning before he had put the paint on.

'Ladies and gentlemen of Bursley, this enlightened and beautiful town which I am now visiting for the first time,' he began in a hard, metallic voice, employing again with the glib accuracy of a machine the exact phrases which he had been using all day, 'look at me—look well at me. How old do you think I am? How old do I seem? Twenty, my dear, do you say?' and he turned with practised insolence to a pot-girl in a red shawl who could not have uttered an audible word to save her soul, but who blushed and giggled with pleasure at this mark of attention. 'Ah! you flatter, fair maiden! I look more than twenty, but I think I may say that I do not look thirty. Does any lady or gentleman think I look thirty? No! As a matter of fact, I was twenty-nine years of age when, in South America, while exploring the ruins of the most ancient civilization of the world—of the world, ladies and gentlemen—I made my wonderful discovery, the Elixir of Youth!'

'What art blethering at, Licksy?' a drunken man called from the back of the crowd, and the nickname stuck to the great discoverer during the rest of the Wakes.

'That, ladies and gentlemen,' the Inca of Peru continued unperturbed, 'was—seventy-two years ago. I am now a hundred and one years old precisely, and as fresh as a kitten, all along of my marvellous elixir. Far older, for instance, than this good dame here.'

He pointed to an aged and wrinkled woman, in blue cotton and a white mutch, who was placidly smoking a short cutty. This creature, bowed and satiate with monotonous years, took the pipe from her indrawn lips, and asked in a weary, trembling falsetto:

'How many wives hast had?'

'Seventane,' the Inca retorted quickly, dropping at once into broad dialect, 'and now lone and lookin' to wed again. Wilt have me?'

'Nay,' replied the crone. 'I've buried four mysen, and no man o' mine shall bury me.'

There was a burst of laughter, amid which the Inca, taking the crowd archly into his confidence, remarked:

'I've never administered my elixir to any of my wives, ladies and gentlemen. You may blame me, but I freely confess the fact;' and he winked.

'Licksy! Licksy!' the drunken man idiotically chanted.

'And now,' the Inca proceeded, coming at length to the practical part of his ovation, 'see here!' With the rapidity of a conjurer he whipped from his pocket a small bottle, and held it up before the increasing audience. It contained a reddish fluid, which shone bright and rich in the sunlight. 'See here!' he cried magnificently, but he was destined to interruption.

A sudden cry arose of 'Black Jack! Black Jack! 'Tis him! He's caught!' And the Inca's crowd, together with all the other crowds filling the market-place, surged off eastward in a dense, struggling mass.

The cynosure of every eye was a springless clay-cart, which was being slowly driven past the newly-erected 'big house' of Enoch Wood, Esquire, towards the Town Hall. In this cart were two constables, with their painted staves drawn, and between the constables sat a man securely chained—Black Jack of Moorthorne, the mining village which lies over the ridge a mile or so east of Bursley. The captive was a ferocious and splendid young Hercules, tall, with enormous limbs and hands and heavy black brows. He was dressed in his soiled working attire of a collier, the trousers strapped under the knees, and his feet shod in vast clogs. With open throat, small head, great jaws, and bold beady eyes, he looked what he was, the superb brute—the brute reckless of all save the instant satisfaction of his desires. He came of a family of colliers, the most debased class in a lawless district. Jack's father had been a colliery-serf, legally enslaved to his colliery, legally liable to be sold with the colliery as a chattel, and legally bound to bring up all his sons as colliers, until the Act of George III. put an end to this incredible survival from the customs of the Dark Ages. Black Jack was now a hero to the crowd, and knew it, for those vast clogs had kicked a woman to death on the previous day. She was a Moorthorne woman, not his wife, but his sweetheart, older than he; people said that she nagged him, and that he was tired of her. The murderer had hidden for a night, and then, defiantly, surrendered to the watch, and the watch were taking him to the watch-house in the ashlar basement of the Town Hall. The feeble horse between the shafts of the cart moved with difficulty through the press, and often the coloured staves of the constables came down thwack on the heads of heedless youth. At length the cart reached the space between the watch-house and the tent of the Inca of Peru, where it stopped while the constables unlocked a massive door; the prisoner remained proudly in the cart, accepting, with obvious delight, the tribute of cheers and jeers, hoots and shouts, from five thousand mouths.

The Inca of Peru stood at the door of his tent and surveyed Black Jack, who was not more than a few feet away from him.

'Have a glass of my elixir,' he said to the death-dealer; 'no one in this town needs it more than thee, by all accounts. Have a glass, and live for ever. Only sixpence.'

The man in the cart laughed aloud.

'I've nowt on me—not a farden,' he answered, in a strong grating voice.

At that moment a girl, half hidden by the cart, sprang forward, offering something in her outstretched palm to the Inca; but he, misunderstanding her intention, merely glanced with passing interest at her face, and returned his gaze to the prisoner.

'I'll give thee a glass, lad,' he said quickly, 'and then thou canst defy Jack Ketch.'

The crowd yelled with excitement, and the murderer held forth his great hand for the potion. Using every art to enhance the effect of this dramatic advertisement, the Inca of Peru raised his bottle on high, and said in a loud, impressive tone:

'This precious liquid has the property, possessed by no other liquid on earth, of frothing twice. I shall pour it into the glass, and it will froth. Black Jack will drink it, and after he has drunk it will froth again. Observe!'

He uncorked the bottle and filled the glass with the reddish fluid, which after a few seconds duly effervesced, to the vague wonder of the populace. The Inca held the glass till the froth had subsided, and then solemnly gave it to Black Jack.

'Drink!' commanded the Inca.

Black Jack took the draught at a gulp, and instantly flung the glass at the Inca's face. It missed him, however. There were signs of a fracas, but the door of the watch-house swung opportunely open, and Jack was dragged from the cart and hustled within. The crowd, with a crowd's fickleness, turned to other affairs.

That evening the ingenious Inca of Peru did good trade for several hours, but towards eleven o'clock the attraction of the public-houses and of a grand special combined bull and bear beating by moonlight in the large yard of the Cock Inn drew away the circle of his customers until there was none left. He retired inside the tent with several pounds in his pocket and a god's consciousness of having made immortal many of the sons and daughters of Adam.

As he was counting out his gains on the tub of eternal youth by the flicker of a dip, someone lifted the flap of the booth and stealthily entered. He sprang up, fearing robbery with violence, which was sufficiently common during the Wakes; but it was only the young girl who had stood behind the cart when he offered to Black Jack his priceless boon. The Inca had noticed her with increasing interest several times during the evening as she loitered restless near the door of the watch-house.

'What do you want?' he asked her, with the ingratiating affability of the rake who foresees everything.

'Give me a drink.'

'A drink of what, my dear?'

'Licksy.'

He raised the dip, and by its light examined her face. It was a kind of face which carries no provocative signal for nine men out of ten, but which will haunt the tenth: a child's face with a passionate woman's eyes burning and dying in it—black hair, black eyes, thin pale cheeks, equine nostrils, red lips, small ears, and the smallest chin conceivable. He smiled at her, pleased.

'Can you pay for it?' he said pleasantly.

The girl evidently belonged to the poorest class. Her shaggy, uncovered head, lean frame, torn gown, and bare feet, all spoke of hardship and neglect.

'I've a silver groat,' she answered, and closed her small fist tighter.

'A silver groat!' he exclaimed, rather astonished. 'Where did you get that from?'

'He give it me for a-fairing yesterday.'

'Who?'

'Him yonder'—she jerked her head back to indicate the watch-house—'Black Jack.'

'What for?'

'He kissed me,' she said boldly; 'I'm his sweetheart.'

'Eh!' The Inca paused a moment, startled. 'But he killed his sweetheart yesterday.'

'What! Meg!' the girl exclaimed with deep scorn. 'Her weren't his true sweetheart. Her druv him to it. Serve her well right! Owd Meg!'

'How old are you, my dear?'

'Don't know. But feyther said last Wakes I was fourtane. I mun keep young for Jack. He wunna have me if I'm owd.'

'But he'll be hanged, they say.'

She gave a short, satisfied laugh.

'Not now he's drunk Licksy—hangman won't get him. I heard a man say Jack 'd get off wi' twenty year for manslaughter, most like.'

'And you'll wait twenty years for him?'

'Yes,' she said; 'I'll meet him at prison gates. But I mun be young. Give me a drink o' Licksy.'

He drew the red draught in silence, and after it had effervesced offered it to her.

''Tis raight?' she questioned, taking the glass.

The Inca nodded, and, lifting the vessel, she opened her eager lips and became immortal. It was the first time in her life that she had drunk out of a glass, and it would be the last.

Struck dumb by the trusting joy in those profound eyes, the Inca took the empty glass from her trembling hand. Frail organism and prey of love! Passion had surprised her too young. Noon had come before the flower could open. She went out of the tent.

'Wench!' the Inca called after her, 'thy groat!'

She paid him and stood aimless for a second, and then started to cross the roadway. Simultaneously there was a rush and a roar from the Cock yard close by. The raging bull, dragging its ropes, and followed by a crowd of alarmed pursuers, dashed out. The girl was plain in the moonlight. Many others were abroad, but the bull seemed to see nothing but her, and, lowering his huge head, he charged with shut eyes and flung her over the Inca's booth.

'Thou's gotten thy wish: thou'rt young for ever!' the Inca of Peru, made a poet for an instant by this disaster, murmured to himself as he bent with the curious crowd over the corpse.

Black Jack was hanged.

Many years after all this Bursley built itself a new Town Hall (with a spire, and a gold angel on the top in the act of crowning the bailiwick with a gold crown), and began to think about getting up in the world.

MARY WITH THE HIGH HAND

In the front-bedroom of Edward Beechinor's small house in Trafalgar Road the two primary social forces of action and reaction—those forces which under a thousand names and disguises have alternately ruled the world since the invention of politics—were pitted against each other in a struggle rendered futile by the equality of the combatants. Edward Beechinor had his money, his superior age, and the possible advantage of being a dying man; Mark Beechinor had his youth and his devotion to an ideal. Near the window, aloof and apart, stood the strange, silent girl whose aroused individuality was to intervene with such effectiveness on behalf of one of the antagonists. It was early dusk on an autumn day.

'Tell me what it is you want, Edward,' said Mark quietly. 'Let us come to the point.'

'Ay,' said the sufferer, lifting his pale hand from the counterpane, 'I'll tell thee.'

He moistened his lips as if in preparation, and pushed back a tuft of sparse gray hair, damp with sweat.

The physical and moral contrast between these two brothers was complete. Edward was forty-nine, a small, thin, stunted man, with a look of narrow cunning, of petty shrewdness working without imagination. He had been clerk to Lawyer Ford for thirty-five years, and had also furtively practised for himself. During this period his mode of life had never varied, save once, and that only a year ago. At the age of fourteen he sat in a grimy room with an old man on one side of him, a copying-press on the other, and a law-stationer's almanac in front, and he earned half a crown a week. At the age of forty-eight he still sat in the same grimy room (of which the ceiling had meanwhile been whitened three times), with the same copying-press and the almanac of the same law-stationers, and he earned thirty shillings a week. But now he, Edward Beechinor, was the old man, and the indispensable lad of fourteen, who had once been himself, was another lad, perhaps thirtieth of the dynasty of office-boys. Throughout this interminable and sterile desert of time he had drawn the same deeds, issued the same writs, written the same letters, kept the same accounts, lied the same lies, and thought the same thoughts. He had learnt nothing except craft, and forgotten nothing except happiness. He had never married, never loved, never been a rake, nor deviated from respectability. He was a success because he had conceived an object, and by sheer persistence attained it. In the eyes of Bursley people he was a very decent fellow, a steady fellow, a confirmed bachelor, a close un, a knowing customer, a curmudgeon, an excellent clerk, a narrow-minded ass, a good Wesleyan, a thrifty individual, and an intelligent burgess—according to the point of view. The lifelong operation of rigorous habit had sunk him into a groove as deep as the canon of some American river. His ideas on every subject were eternally and immutably fixed, and, without being altogether aware of it, he was part of the solid foundation of England's greatness. In 1892, when the whole of the Five Towns was agitated by the great probate case of Wilbraham v. Wilbraham, in which Mr. Ford acted for the defendants, Beechinor, then aged forty-eight, was torn from his stool and sent out to Rio de Janeiro as part of a commission to take the evidence of an important witness who had declined all offers to come home.

The old clerk was full of pride and self-importance at being thus selected, but secretly he shrank from the journey, the mere idea of which filled him with vague apprehension and alarm. His nature had lost all its adaptability; he trembled like a young girl at the prospect of new experiences. On the return voyage the vessel was quarantined at Liverpool for a fortnight, and Beechinor had an attack of low fever. Eight months afterwards he was ill again. Beechinor went to bed for the last time, cursing Providence, Wilbraham *v.* Wilbraham, and Rio.

Mark Beechinor was thirty, just nineteen years younger than his brother. Tall, uncouth, big-boned, he had a rather ferocious and forbidding aspect; yet all women seemed to like him, despite the fact that he seldom could open his mouth to them. There must have been something in his wild and liquid dark eyes which mutely appealed for their protective sympathy, something about him of shy and wistful romance that atoned for the huge awkwardness of this taciturn elephant. Mark was at present the manager of a small china manufactory at Longshaw, the farthest of the Five Towns in Staffordshire, and five miles from Bursley. He was an exceptionally clever potter, but he never made money. He had the dreamy temperament of the inventor. He was a man of ideas, the kind of man who is capable of forgetting that he has not had his dinner, and who can live apparently content amid the grossest domestic neglect. He had once spoilt a hundred and fifty pounds' worth of ware by firing it in a new kiln of his own contrivance; it cost him three years of atrocious parsimony to pay for the ware and the building of the kiln. He was impulsively and recklessly charitable, and his Saturday afternoons and Sundays were chiefly devoted to the passionate propagandism of the theories of liberty, equality, and fraternity.

'Is it true as thou'rt for marrying Sammy Mellor's daughter over at Hanbridge?' Edward Beechinor asked, in the feeble, tremulous voice of one agonized by continual pain.

Among relatives and acquaintances he commonly spoke the Five Towns dialect, reserving the other English for official use.

Mark stood at the foot of the bed, leaning with his elbows on the brass rail. Like most men, he always felt extremely nervous and foolish in a sick-room, and the delicacy of this question, so bluntly put, added to his embarrassment. He looked round timidly in the direction of the girl at the window; her back was towards him.

'It's possible,' he replied. 'I haven't asked her yet.'

'Her'll have no money?'

'No.'

'Thou'lt want some brass to set up with. Look thee here, Mark: I made my will seven years ago i' thy favour.'

'Thank ye,' said Mark gratefully.

'But that,' the dying man continued with a frown—'that was afore thou'dst taken up with these socialistic doctrines o' thine. I've heard as thou'rt going to be th' secretary o' the Hanbridge Labour Church, as they call it.'

Hanbridge is the metropolis of the Five Towns, and its Labour Church is the most audacious and influential of all the local activities, half secret, but relentlessly determined, whose aim is to establish the new democratic heaven and the new democratic earth by means of a gradual and bloodless revolution. Edward Beechinor uttered its abhorred name with a bitter and scornful hatred characteristic of the Toryism of a man who, having climbed high up out of the crowd, fiercely resents any widening or smoothing of the difficult path which he himself has conquered.

'They've asked me to take the post,' Mark answered.

'What's the wages?' the older man asked, with exasperated sarcasm.

'Nothing.'

'Mark, lad,' the other said, softening, 'I'm worth seven hundred pounds and this freehold house. What dost think o' that?'

Even in that moment, with the world and its riches slipping away from his dying grasp, the contemplation of this great achievement of thrift filled Edward Beechinor with a sublime satisfaction. That sum of seven hundred pounds, which many men would dissipate in a single night, and forget the next morning that they had done so, seemed vast and almost incredible to him.

'I know you've always been very careful,' said Mark politely.

'Give up this old Labour Church'—again old Beechinor laid a withering emphasis on the phrase—'give up this Labour Church, and its all thine—house and all.'

Mark shook his head.

'Think twice,' the sick man ordered angrily. 'I tell thee thou'rt standing to lose every shilling.'

'I must manage without it, then.'

A silence fell.

Each brother was absolutely immovable in his decision, and the other knew it. Edward might have said: 'I am a dying man: give up this thing to oblige me.' And Mark could have pleaded: 'At such a moment I would do anything to oblige you—except this, and this I really can't do. Forgive me.' Such amenities would possibly have eased the cord which was about to snap; but the idea of regarding Edward's condition as a factor in the case did not suggest itself favourably to the grim Beechinor stock, so stern, harsh, and rude. The sick man wiped from his sunken features the sweat which continually gathered there. Then he turned upon his side with a grunt.

'Thou must fetch th' lawyer,' he said at length, 'for I'll cut thee off.'

It was a strange request—like ordering a condemned man to go out and search for his executioner; but Mark answered with perfect naturalness:

'Yes. Mr. Ford, I suppose?'

'Ford? No! Dost think I want *him* meddling i' my affairs? Go to young Baines up th' road. Tell him to come at once. He's sure to be at home, as it's Saturday night.'

'Very well.'

Mark turned to leave the room.

'And, young un, I've done with thee. Never pass my door again till thou know'st I'm i' my coffin. Understand?'

Mark hesitated a moment, and then went out, quietly closing the door. No sooner had he done so than the girl, hitherto so passive at the window, flew after him.

There are some women whose calm, enigmatic faces seem always to suggest the infinite. It is given to few to know them, so rare as they are, and their lives usually so withdrawn; but sometimes they pass in the street, or sit like sphinxes in the church or the theatre, and then the memory of their features, persistently recurring, troubles us for days. They are peculiar to no class, these women: you may find them in a print gown or in diamonds. Often they have thin, rather long lips and deep rounded chins; but it is the fine upward curve of the nostrils and the fall of the eyelids which most surely mark them. Their glances and their faint smiles are beneficent, yet with a subtle shade of half-malicious superiority. When they look at you from under those apparently fatigued eyelids, you feel that they have an inward and concealed existence far beyond the ordinary—that they are aware of many things which you can never know. It is as though their souls, during former incarnations, had trafficked with the secret forces of nature, and so acquired a mysterious and nameless quality above all the transient attributes of beauty, wit, and talent. They exist: that is enough; that is their genius. Whether they control, or are at the mercy of, those secret forces; whether they have in fact learnt, but may not speak, the true answer to the eternal Why; whether they are not perhaps a riddle even to their own simple selves: these are points which can never be decided.

Everyone who knew Mary Beechinor, in her cousin's home, or at chapel, or on Titus Price's earthenware manufactory, where she worked, said or thought that 'there was something about her ...' and left the phrase unachieved. She was twenty-five, and she had lived under the same roof with Edward Beechinor for seven years, since the sudden death of her parents. The arrangement then made was that Edward should keep her, while she conducted his household. She had insisted on permission to follow her own occupation, and in order that she might be at liberty to do so she personally paid eighteenpence a week to a little girl who came in to perform sundry necessary duties every day at noon. Mary Beechinor was a paintress by trade. As a class the paintresses of the Five Towns are somewhat similar to the more famous mill-girls of Lancashire and Yorkshire—fiercely independent by reason of good wages earned, loving finery and brilliant colours, loud-tongued and aggressive, perhaps, and for the rest neither more nor less kindly, passionate, faithful, than any other Saxon women anywhere. The paintresses, however, have some slight advantage over the mill-girls in the outward reticences of demeanour, due no doubt to the fact that their ancient craft demands a higher skill, and is pursued under more humane and tranquil conditions. Mary Beechinor worked in the 'band-and-line' department of the painting-shop at Price's. You may have observed the geometrical exactitude of the broad and thin coloured lines round the edges of a common cup and saucer, and speculated upon the means by which it was arrived at. A girl drew those lines, a girl with a hand as sure as Giotto's, and no better tools than a couple of brushes and a small revolving table called a whirler. Forty-eight hours a week Mary Beechinor sat before her whirler. Actuating the treadle, she placed a piece of ware on the flying disc, and with a single unerring flip of the finger pushed it precisely to the centre; then she held the full brush firmly against the ware, and in three seconds the band encircled it truly; another brush taken up, and the line below the band also stood complete. And this process was repeated, with miraculous swiftness, hour after hour, week after week, year after year. Mary could decorate over thirty dozen cups and saucers in a day, at three halfpence the dozen. 'Doesn't she ever do anything else?' some visitor might curiously inquire, whom Titus Price was showing over his ramshackle manufactory. 'No, always the same thing,' Titus would answer, made proud for the moment of this phenomenon of stupendous monotony. 'I wonder how she can stand it—she has a refined face,' the visitor might remark; and Mary Beechinor was left alone again. The idea that her work was monotonous probably never occurred to the girl. It was her work—as natural as sleep, or the knitting which she always did in the dinner-hour. The calm and silent regularity of it had become part of her, deepening her original quiescence, and setting its seal upon her inmost spirit. She was not in the fellowship of the other girls in the painting-shop. She seldom joined their more boisterous diversions, nor talked their talk, and she never manoeuvred for their men. But they liked her, and their attitude showed a certain respect, forced from them by they knew not what. The powers in the office spoke of Mary Beechinor as 'a very superior girl.'

She ran downstairs after Mark, and he waited in the narrow hall, where there was scarcely room for two people to pass. Mark looked at her inquiringly. Rather thin, and by no means tall, she seemed the merest morsel by his side. She was wearing her second-best crimson merino frock, partly to receive the doctor and partly because it was Saturday night; over this a plain bibless apron. Her cold gray eyes faintly sparkled in anger above the cheeks white with watching, and the dropped corners of her mouth showed a contemptuous indignation. Mary Beechinor was ominously roused from the accustomed calm of years. Yet Mark at first had no suspicion that she was disturbed. To him that pale and inviolate face, even while it cast a spell over him, gave no sign of the fires within.

She took him by the coat-sleeve and silently directed him into the gloomy little parlour crowded with mahogany and horsehair furniture, white antimacassars, wax flowers under glass, and ponderous gilt-clasped Bibles.

'It's a cruel shame!' she whispered, as though afraid of being overheard by the dying man upstairs.

'Do you think I ought to have given way?' he questioned, reddening.

'You mistake me,' she said quickly; and with a sudden movement she went up to him and put her hand on his shoulder. The caress, so innocent, unpremeditated, and instinctive, ran through him like a voltaic shock. These two were almost strangers; they had scarcely met till within the past week, Mark being seldom in Bursley. 'You mistake me—it is a shame of *him*! I'm fearfully angry.'

'Angry?' he repeated, astonished.

'Yes, angry.' She walked to the window, and, twitching at the blind-cord, gazed into the dim street. It was beginning to grow dark. 'Shall you fetch the lawyer? I shouldn't if I were you. I won't.'

'I must fetch him,' Mark said.

She turned round and admired him. 'What *will* he do with his precious money?' she murmured.

'Leave it to you, probably.'

'Not he. I wouldn't touch it—not now; it's yours by rights. Perhaps you don't know that when I came here it was distinctly understood I wasn't to expect anything under his will. Besides, I have my own money ... Oh dear! If he wasn't in such pain, wouldn't I talk to him—for the first and last time in my life!'

'You must please not say a word to him. I don't really want the money.'

'But you ought to have it. If he takes it away from you he's *unjust*.'

'What did the doctor say this afternoon?' asked Mark, wishing to change the subject.

'He said the crisis would come on Monday, and when it did Edward would be dead all in a minute. He said it would be just like taking prussic acid.'

'Not earlier than Monday?'

'He said he thought Monday.'

'Of course I shall take no notice of what Edward said to me—I shall call to-morrow morning—and stay. Perhaps he won't mind seeing me. And then you can tell me what happens to-night.'

'I'm sure I shall send that lawyer man about his business,' she threatened.

'Look here,' said Mark timorously as he was leaving the house, 'I've told you I don't want the money—I would give it away to some charity; but do you think I ought to pretend to yield, just to humour him, and let him die quiet and peaceful? I shouldn't like him to die hating——'

'Never—never!' she exclaimed.

'What have you and Mark been talking about?' asked Edward Beechinor apprehensively as Mary re-entered the bedroom.

'Nothing,' she replied with a grave and soothing kindliness of tone.

'Because, miss, if you think——'

'You must have your medicine now, Edward.'

But before giving the patient his medicine she peeped through the curtain and watched Mark's figure till it disappeared up the hill towards Bleakridge. He, on his part, walked with her image always in front of him. He thought hers was the strongest, most righteous soul he had ever encountered; it seemed as if she had a perfect passion for truth and justice. And a week ago he had deemed her a capable girl, certainly—but lackadaisical!

The clock had struck ten before Mr. Baines, the solicitor, knocked at the door. Mary hesitated, and then took him upstairs in silence while he suavely explained to her why he had been unable to come earlier. This lawyer was a young Scotsman who had descended upon the town from nowhere, bought a small decayed practice, and within two years had transformed it into a large and flourishing business by one of those feats of energy, audacity, and tact, combined, of which some Scotsmen seem to possess the secret.

'Here is Mr. Baines, Edward,' Mary said quietly; and then, having rearranged the sick man's pillow, she vanished out of the room and went into the kitchen.

The gas-jet there showed only a point of blue, but she did not turn it up. Dragging an old oak rush-seated rocking-chair near to the range, where a scrap of fire still glowed, she rocked herself gently in the darkness.

After about half an hour Mr. Baines's voice sounded at the head of the stairs:

'Miss Beechinor, will ye kindly step up? We shall want some asseestance.'

She obeyed, but not instantly.

In the bedroom Mr. Baines, a fountain-pen between his fine white teeth, was putting some coal on the fire. He stood up as she entered.

'Mr. Beechinor is about to make a new will,' he said, without removing the pen from his mouth, 'and ye will kindly witness it.'

The small room appeared to be full of Baines—he was so large and fleshy and assertive. The furniture, even the chest of drawers, was dwarfed into toy-furniture, and Beechinor, slight and shrunken-up, seemed like a cadaverous manikin in the bed.

'Now, Mr. Beechinor.' Dusting his hands, the lawyer took a newly-written document from the dressing-table, and, spreading it on the lid of a cardboard box, held it before the dying man. 'Here's the pen. There! I'll help ye to hold it.'

Beechinor clutched the pen. His wrinkled and yellow face, flushed in irregular patches as though the cheeks had been badly rouged, was covered with perspiration, and each difficult movement, even to the slightest lifting of the head, showed extreme exhaustion. He cast at Mary a long sinister glance of mistrust and apprehension.

'What is there in this will?'

Mr. Baines looked sharply up at the girl, who now stood at the side of the bed opposite him. Mechanically she smoothed the tumbled bed-clothes.

'That's nowt to do wi' thee, lass,' said Beechinor resentfully.

'It isn't necessary that a witness to a will should be aware of its contents,' said Baines. 'In fact, it's quite unusual.'

'I sign nothing in the dark,' she said, smiling. Through their half-closed lids her eyes glimmered at Baines.

'Ha! Legal caution acquired from your cousin, I presume.' Baines smiled at her. 'But let me assure ye, Miss Beechinor, this is a mere matter of form. A will must be signed in the presence of two witnesses, both present at the same time; and there's only yeself and me for it.'

Mary looked at the dying man, whose features were writhed in pain, and shook her head.

'Tell her,' he murmured with bitter despair, and sank down into the pillows, dropping the fountain-pen, which had left a stain of ink on the sheet before Baines could pick it up.

'Well, then, Miss Beechinor, if ye must know,' Baines began with sarcasm, 'the will is as follows: The testator—that's Mr. Beechinor—leaves twenty guineas to his brother Mark to show that he bears him no ill-will and forgives him. The rest of his estate is to be realized, and the proceeds given to the North Staffordshire Infirmary, to found a bed, which is to be called the Beechinor bed. If there is any surplus, it is to go to the Law Clerks' Provident Society. That is all.'

'I shall have nothing to do with it,' Mary said coldly.

'Young lady, we don't want ye to have anything to do with it. We only desire ye to witness the signature.'

'I won't witness the signature, and I won't see it signed.'

'Damn thee, Mary! thou'rt a wicked wench,' Beechinor whispered in hoarse, feeble tones. He saw himself robbed of the legitimate fruit of all those interminable years of toilsome thrift. This girl by a trick would prevent him from disposing of his own. He, Edward Beechinor, shrewd and wealthy, was being treated like a child. He was too weak to rave, but from his aggrieved and furious heart he piled silent curses on her. 'Go, fetch another witness,' he added to the lawyer.

'Wait a moment,' said Baines. 'Miss Beechinor, do ye mean to say that ye will cross the solemn wish of a dying man?'

'I mean to say I won't help a dying man to commit a crime.'

'A crime?'

'Yes,' she answered, 'a crime. Seven years ago Mr. Beechinor willed everything to his brother Mark, and Mark ought to have everything. Mark is his only brother—his only relation except me. And Edward knows it isn't me wants any of his money. North Staffordshire Infirmary indeed! It's a crime!... What business have *you*,' she went on to Edward Beechinor, 'to punish Mark just because his politics aren't——'

'That's beside the point,' the lawyer interrupted. 'A testator has a perfect right to leave his property as he chooses, without giving reasons. Now, Miss Beechinor, I must ask ye to be judeecious.'

Mary shut her lips.

'Her'll never do it. I tell thee, fetch another witness.'

The old man sprang up in a sort of frenzy as he uttered the words, and then fell back in a brief swoon.

Mary wiped his brow, and pushed away the wet and matted hair. Presently he opened his eyes, moaning. Mr. Baines folded up the will, put it in his pocket, and left the room with quick steps. Mary heard him open the front-door and then return to the foot of the stairs.

'Miss Beechinor,' he called, 'I'll speak with ye a moment.'

She went down.

'Do you mind coming into the kitchen?' she said, preceding him and turning up the gas; 'there's no light in the front-room.'

He leaned up against the high mantelpiece; his frock-coat hung to the level of the oven-knob. She had one hand on the white deal table. Between them a tortoiseshell cat purred on the red-tiled floor.

'Ye're doing a verra serious thing, Miss Beechinor. As Mr. Beechinor's solicitor, I should just like to be acquaint with the real reasons for this conduct.'

'I've told you.' She had a slightly quizzical look.

'Now, as to Mark,' the lawyer continued blandly, 'Mr. Beechinor explained the whole circumstances to me. Mark as good as defied his brother.'

'That's nothing to do with it.'

'By the way, it appears that Mark is practically engaged to be married. May I ask if the lady is yeself?'

She hesitated.

'If so,' he proceeded, 'I may tell ye informally that I admire the pluck of ye. But, nevertheless, that will has got to be executed.'

'The young lady is a Miss Mellor of Hanbridge.'

'I'm going to fetch my clerk,' he said shortly. 'I can see ye're an obstinate and unfathomable woman. I'll be back in half an hour.'

When he had departed she bolted the front door top and bottom, and went upstairs to the dying man.

Nearly an hour elapsed before she heard a knock. Mr. Baines had had to arouse his clerk from sleep. Instead of going down to the front-door, Mary threw up the bedroom window and looked out. It was a mild but starless night. Trafalgar Road was silent save for the steam-car, which, with its load of revellers returning from Hanbridge—that centre of gaiety—slipped rumbling down the hill towards Bursley.

'What do you want—disturbing a respectable house at this time of night?' she called in a loud whisper when the car had passed. 'The door's bolted, and I can't come down. You must come in the morning.'

'Miss Beechinor, ye will let us in—I charge ye.'

'It's useless, Mr. Baines.'

'I'll break the door down. I'm a strong man, and a determined. Ye are carrying things too far.'

In another moment the two men heard the creak of the bolts. Mary stood before them, vaguely discernible, but a forbidding figure.

'If you must—come upstairs,' she said coldly.

'Stay here in the passage, Arthur,' said Mr. Baines; 'I'll call ye when I want ye;' and he followed Mary up the stairs.

Edward Beechinor lay on his back, and his sunken eyes stared glassily at the ceiling. The skin of his emaciated face, stretched tightly over the protruding bones, had lost all its crimson, and was green, white, yellow. The mouth was wide open. His drawn features wore a terribly sardonic look—a purely physical effect of the disease; but it seemed to the two spectators that this mean and disappointed slave of a miserly habit had by one superb imaginative effort realized the full vanity of all human wishes and pretensions.

'Ye can go; I shan't want ye,' said Mr. Baines, returning to the clerk.

The lawyer never spoke of that night's business. Why should he? To what end? Mark Beechinor, under the old will, inherited the seven hundred pounds and the house. Miss Mellor of Hanbridge is still Miss Mellor, her hand not having been formally sought. But Mark, secretary of the Labour Church, is married. Miss Mellor, with a quite pardonable air of tolerant superiority, refers to his wife as 'a strange, timid little creature—she couldn't say Bo to a goose.'

THE DOG

This is a scandalous story. It scandalized the best people in Bursley; some of them would wish it forgotten. But since I have begun to tell it I may as well finish. Moreover, like most tales whispered behind fans and across club-tables, it carries a high and valuable moral. The moral—I will let you have it at once—is that those who love in glass houses should pull down the blinds.

I

He had got his collar on safely; it bore his name—Ellis Carter. Strange name for a dog, perhaps; and perhaps it was even more strange that his collar should be white. But such dogs are not common dogs. He tied his necktie exquisitely; caressed his hair again with two brushes; curved his young moustache, and then assumed his waistcoat and his coat; the trousers had naturally preceded the collar. He beheld the suit in the glass, and saw that it was good. And it was not built in London, either. There are tailors in Bursley. And in particular there is the dog's tailor. Ask the dog's tailor, as the dog once did, whether he can really do as well as London, and he will smile on you with gentle pity; he will not stoop to utter the obvious Yes. He may casually inform you that, if he is not in London himself, the explanation is that he has reasons for preferring Bursley. He is the social equal of all his clients. He belongs to the dogs' club. He knows, and everybody knows, that he is a first-class tailor with a first-class connection, and no dog would dare to condescend to him. He is a great creative artist; the dogs who wear his clothes may be said to interpret his creations. Now, Ellis was a great interpretative artist, and the tailor recognised the fact. When the tailor met Ellis on Duck Bank greatly wearing a new suit, the scene was impressive. It was as though Elgar had stopped to hear Paderewski play 'Pomp and Circumstance' on the piano.

Ellis descended from his bedroom into the hall, took his straw hat, chose a stick, and went out into the portico of the new large house on the Hawkins, near Oldcastle. In the neighbourhood of the Five Towns no road is more august, more correct, more detached, more umbrageous, than the Hawkins. M.P.'s live there. It is the link between the aristocratic and antique aloofness of Oldcastle and the solid commercial prosperity of the Five Towns. Ellis adorned the portico. Young (a bare twenty-two), fair, handsome, smiling, graceful, well-built, perfectly groomed, he was an admirable and a characteristic specimen of the race of dogs which, with the modern growth of luxury and the Luxurious Spirit, has become so marked a phenomenon in the social development of the once barbarous Five Towns.

When old Jack Carter (reputed to be the best turner that Bursley ever produced) started a little potbank near St. Peter's Church in 1861—he was then forty, and had saved two hundred pounds—he little dreamt that the supreme and final result after forty years would be the dog. But so it was. Old Jack Carter had a son John Carter, who married at twenty-five and lived at first on twenty-five shillings a week, and enthusiastically continued the erection of the fortune which old Jack had begun. At thirty-three, after old Jack's death, John became a Town Councillor. At thirty-six he became Mayor and the father of Ellis, and the recipient of a silver cradle. Ellis was his wife's maiden name. At forty-two he built the finest earthenware manufactory in Bursley, down by the canal-side at Shawport. At fifty-two he had been everything that a man can be in the Five Towns—from County Councillor to President of the Society for the Prosecution of Felons. Then Ellis left school and came to the works to carry on the tradition, and his father suddenly discovered him. The truth was that John Carter had been so laudably busy with the affairs of his town and county that he had nearly forgotten his family. Ellis, in the process of achieving doghood, soon taught his father a thing or two. And John learnt. John could manage a public meeting, but he could not manage Ellis. Besides, there was plenty of money; and Ellis was so ingratiating, and had curly hair that somehow won sympathy. And, after all, Ellis was not such a duffer as all that at the works. John knew other people's sons who were worse. And Ellis could keep order in the paintresses' 'shops' as order had never been kept there before.

John sometimes wondered what old Jack would have said about Ellis and his friends, those handsome dogs, those fine dandies, who taught to the Five Towns the virtue of grace and of style and of dash, who went up to London—some of them even went to Paris—and brought back civilization to the Five Towns, who removed from the Five Towns the reproach of being uncouth and behind the times. Was the outcome of two generations of unremitting toil merely Ellis? (Ellis had several pretty sisters, but they did not count.) John could only guess at what old Jack's attitude might have been towards Ellis—Ellis, who had his shirts made to measure. He knew exactly what was Ellis's attitude towards the ideals of old Jack, old Jack the class leader, who wore clogs till he was thirty, and dined in his shirt-sleeves at one o'clock to the end of his life.

Ellis quitted the portico, ran down the winding garden-path, and jumped neatly and fearlessly on to an electric tramcar as it passed at the rate of fifteen miles an hour. The car was going to Hanbridge, and it was crowded with the joy of life; Ellis had to stand on the step. This was the Saturday before the first Monday in August, and therefore the formal opening of Knype Wakes, the most carnivalesque of all the carnivals which enliven the four seasons in the Five Towns. It is still called Knype Wakes, because once Knype overshadowed Hanbridge in importance; but its headquarters are now quite properly at Hanbridge, the hub, the centre, the Paris of the Five Towns—Hanbridge, the county borough of sixty odd thousand inhabitants. It is the festival of the masses that old Jack sprang from, and every genteel person who can leaves the Five Towns for the seaside at the end of July. Nevertheless, the district is never more crammed than at Knype Wakes. And, of course, genteel persons, whom circumstances have forced to remain in the Five Towns, sally out in the evening to 'do' the Wakes in a spirit of tolerant condescension. Ellis was in this case. His parents and sisters were at Llandudno, and he had been left in charge of the works and of the new house. He was always free; he could always pity the bondage of his sisters; but now he was more free than ever—he was absolutely free. Imagine the delicious feeling that surged in his heart as he prepared to plunge himself doggishly into the wild ocean of the Wakes. By the way, in that heart was the image of a girl.

II

He stepped off the car on the outskirts of Hanbridge, and strolled gently and spectacularly into the joyous town. The streets became more and more crowded and noisy as he approached the market-place, and in Crown Square tramcars from the four quarters of the earth discharged tramloads of humanity at the rate of two a minute, and then glided off again empty in search of more humanity. The lower portion of Crown Square was devoted to tramlines; in the upper portion the Wakes began, and spread into the market-place, and thence by many tentacles into all manner of streets.

No Wakes is better than Knype Wakes; that is to say, no Wakes is more ear-splitting, more terrific, more dizzying, or more impassable. When you go to Knype Wakes you get stuck in the midst of an enormous crowd, and you see roundabouts, swings, switchbacks, myrioramas, atrocity booths, quack dentists, shooting-galleries, cocoanut-shies, and bazaars, all around you. Every establishment is jewelled, gilded, and electrically lighted; every establishment has an orchestra, most often played by steam and conducted by a stoker; every establishment has a steam—whistle, which shrieks at the beginning and at the end of each round or performance. You stand fixed in the multitude listening to a thousand orchestras and whistles, with the roar of machinery and the merry din of car-bells, and the popping of rifles for a background of noise. Your eyes are charmed by the whirling of a million lights and the mad whirling of millions of beautiful girls and happy youths under the lights. For the roundabouts rule the scene; the roundabouts take the money. The supreme desire of the revellers is to describe circles, either on horseback or in yachts, either simple circles or complex circles, either up and down or straight along, but always circles. And it is as though inventors had sat up at nights puzzling their brains how best to make revellers seasick while keeping them equidistant from a steam-orchestra.... Then the crowd solidly lurches, and you find yourself up against a dentist, or a firm of wrestlers, or a roundabout, or an ice-cream refectory, and you take what comes. You have begun to 'do' the Wakes. The splendid insanity seizes you. The lights, the colours, the explosions, the shrieks, the feathered hats, the pretty faces as they fly past, the gilding, the statuary, the August night, and the mingling of a thousand melodies in a counterpoint beyond the dreams of Wagner—these things have stirred the sap of life in you, have shown you how fine it is to be alive, and, careless and free, have caught up your spirit into a heaven from which you scornfully survey the year of daily toil between one Wakes and another as the eagle scornfully surveys the potato-field. Your nostrils dilate—nay, matters reach such a pass that, even if you are genteel, you forget to condescend.

III

After Ellis had had the correct drink in the private bar up the passage at the Turk's Head, and after he had plunged into the crowd and got lost in it, and submitted good-humouredly to the frequent ordeal of the penny squirt as administered by adorable creatures in bright skirts, he found himself cast up by the human ocean on the macadam shore near a shooting-gallery. This was no ordinary shooting-gallery. It was one of Jenkins's affairs (Jenkins of Manchester), and on either side of it Jenkins's Venetian gondolas and Jenkins's Mexican mustangs were whizzing round two of Jenkins's orchestras at twopence a time, and taking thirty-two pounds an hour. This gallery was very different from the old galleries, in which you leaned against a brass bar and shot up a kind of a drain. This gallery was a large and brilliant room, with the front-wall taken out. It was hung with mirrors and cretonnes, it was richly carpeted, and, of course, it was lighted by electricity. Carved and gilded tables bore a whole armoury of weapons. You shot at tobacco-pipes, twisting and stationary, at balls poised on jets of water, and at proper targets. In the corners of the saloon, near the open, were large crimson plush lounges, on which you lounged after the fatigue of shooting.

A pink-clad girl, young and radiant, had the concern in charge.

She was speeding a party of bankrupt shooters, when she caught sight of Ellis. Ellis answered her smile, and strolled up to the booth with a countenance that might have meant anything. You can never tell what a dog is thinking.

"Ello!' said the girl prettily (or, rather, she shouted prettily, having to compete with the two orchestras). 'You here again?'

The truth was that Ellis had been there on the previous night, when the Wakes was only half opened, and he had come again to-night expressly in order to see her; but he would not have admitted, even to himself, that he had come expressly in order to see her; in his mind it was just a chance that he might see her. She was a jolly girl. (We are gradually approaching the scandalous part.)

'What a jolly frock!' he said, when he had shot five celluloid balls in succession off a jet of water.

Smiling, she mechanically took a ball out of the basket and let it roll down the conduit to the fountain.

'Do you think so?' she replied, smoothing the fluffy muslin apron with her small hands, black from contact with the guns. 'That one I wore last night was my second-best. I only wear this on Saturdays and Mondays.'

He nodded like a connoisseur. The sixth ball had sprung up to the top of the jet. He removed it with the certainty of a King's Prize winner, and she complimented him.

'Ah!' he said, 'you should have seen me before I took to smoking and drinking!'

She laughed freely. She was always showing her fine teeth. And she had such a frank, jolly countenance, not exactly pretty—better than pretty. She was a little short and a little plump, and she wore a necklace round her neck, a ring on her dainty, dirty finger, and a watch-bracelet on her wrist.

'Why!' she exclaimed. 'How old are you?'

'How old are *you*?' he retorted.

Dogs do not give things away like that.

'I'm nineteen,' she said submissively. 'At least, I shall be come Martinmas.'
And she yawned.

'Well,' he said, 'a little girl like you ought to be in bed.'

'Sunday to-morrow,' she observed.

'Aren't you glad you're English?' he remarked. 'If you were in Paris you'd have
to work Sundays too.'

'Not me!' she said. 'Who told you that? Have you been to Paris?'

'No,' he admitted cautiously; 'but a friend of mine has, and he told me. He
came back only last week, and he says they keep open Sundays, and all night
sometimes. Sunday is the great day over there.'

'Well,' said the girl kindly, 'don't you believe it. The police wouldn't allow it. I
know what the police are.'

More shooters entered the saloon. Ellis had finished his dozen; he sank into a
lounge, and elegantly lighted a cigarette, and watched her serve the other
marksmen. She was decidedly charming, and so jolly—with him. He noticed with
satisfaction that with the other marksmen she showed a certain high reserve.

They did not stay long, and when they were gone she came across to the
lounge and gazed at him provocatively.

'Dashed if she hasn't taken a fancy to me!'

The thought ran through him like lightning.

'Well?' she said.

'What do you do with yourself Sundays?' he asked her.

'Oh, sleep.'

'All day?'

'All morning.'

'What do you do in the afternoon?'

'Oh, nothing.'

She laughed gaily.

'Come out with me, eh?'

'To-morrow? Oh, I should LOVE TO!' she cried.

Her voice expanded into large capitals because by a singular chance both the
neighbouring orchestras stopped momentarily together, and thus gave her shout a
fair field. The effect was startling. It startled Ellis. He had not for an instant
expected that she would consent. Never, dog though he was, had he armed a girl
out on any afternoon, to say nothing of Sunday afternoon, and Knype's Wakes
Sunday at that! He had talked about girls at the club. He understood the theory.
But the practice——

The foundation of England's greatness is that Englishmen hate to look fools.
The fear of being taken for a ninny will spur an Englishman to the most
surprising deeds of courage. Ellis said 'Good!' with apparent enthusiasm, and
arranged to be waiting for her at half-past two at the Turk's Head. Then he left
the saloon and struck out anew into the ocean. He wanted to think it over.

Once, painful to relate, he had thoughts of failing to keep the appointment. However, she was so jolly and frank. And what a fancy she must have taken to him! No, he would see it through.

IV

If anybody had prophesied to Ellis that he would be driving out a Wakes girl in a dogcart that Sunday afternoon he would have laughed at the prophet; but so it occurred. He arrived at the Turk's Head at two twenty-five. She was there before him, dressed all in blue, except the white shoes and stockings, weighing herself on the machine in the yard. She showed her teeth, told him she weighed nine stone one, and abruptly asked him if he could drive. He said he could. She clapped her hands and sprang off the machine. Her father had bought a new mare the day before, and it was in the Turk's Head stable, and the yardman said it wanted exercise, and there was a dogcart and harness idling about, and, in short, Ellis should drive her to Sneyd Park, which she had long desired to see.

Ellis wished to ask questions, but the moment did not seem auspicious.

In a few minutes the new mare, a high and somewhat frisky bay, with big shoulders, was in the shafts of a high, green dogcart. When asked if he could drive, Ellis ought to have answered: 'That depends—on the horse.' Many men can tool a fifteen-year-old screw down a country lane who would hesitate to get up behind a five-year-old animal (in need of exercise) for a spin down Broad Street, Hanbridge, on Knype Wakes Sunday. Ellis could drive; he could just drive. His father had always steadfastly refused to keep horses, but the fathers of other dogs were more progressive, and Ellis had had opportunities. He knew how to take the reins, and get up, and give the office; indeed, he had read a handbook on the subject. So he took the reins and got up, and the Wakes girl got up.

He chirruped. The mare merely backed.

'Give 'er 'er mouth,' said the yardman disgustedly.

'Oh!' said Ellis, and slackened the reins, and the mare pawed forward.

Then he had to turn her in the yard, and get her and the dogcart down the passage. He doubted whether he should do it, for the passage seemed a size too small. However, he did it, or the mare did it, and the entire organism swerved across a portion of the footpath into Broad Street.

For quite a quarter of a mile down Broad Street Ellis blushed, and kept his gaze between the mare's ears. However, the mare went beautifully. You could have driven her with a silken thread, so it seemed. And then the dog, growing accustomed to his prominence up there on the dogcart, began to be a bit doggy. He knew the little thing's age and weight, but, really, when you take a girl out for a Sunday spin you want more information about her than that. Her asked her name, and her name was Jenkins—Ada. She was the great Jenkins's daughter.

('Oh,' thought Ellis, 'the deuce you are!')

'Father's gone to Manchester for the day, and aunt's looking after me,' said Ada.

'Do they know you've come out—like this?'

'Not much!' She laughed deliciously. 'How lovely it is!'

At Knype they drew up before the Five Towns Hotel and descended. The Five Towns Hotel is the greatest hotel in North Staffordshire. It has two hundred rooms. It would not entirely disgrace Northumberland Avenue. In the Five

Towns it is august, imposing, and unique. They had a lemonade there, and proceeded. A clock struck; it was a near thing. No more refreshments now until they had passed the three-mile limit!

Yes! Not two hundred yards further on she spied an ice-cream shop in Fleet Road, and Ellis learnt that she adored ice-cream. The mare waited patiently outside in the thronged street.

After that the pilgrimage to Sneyd was punctuated with ice-creams. At the Stag at Sneyd (where, among ninety-and-nine dogcarts, Ellis's dogcart was the brightest green of them all) Ada had another lemonade, and Ellis had something else. They saw the Park, and Ada giggled charmingly her appreciation of its beauty. The conversation throughout consisted chiefly of Ada's teeth. Ellis said he would return by a different route, and he managed to get lost. How anyone driving to Hanbridge from Sneyd could arrive at the mining village of Silverton is a mystery. But Ellis arrived there, and he ultimately came out at Hillport, the aristocratic suburb of Bursley, where he had always lived till the last year. He feared recognition there, and his fear was justified. Some silly ass, a schoolmate, cried, 'Go it!' as the machine bowled along, and the mischief was that the mare, startled, went it. She went it down the curving hill, and the vehicle after her, like a kettle tied to a dog's tail.

Ellis winked stoutly at Ada when they reached the bottom, and gave the mare a piece of his mind, to which she objected. As they crossed the railway-bridge a goods-train ran underneath and puffed smoke into the mare's eyes. She set her ears back.

'Would you!' cried Ellis authoritatively, and touched her with the whip (he had forgotten the handbook).

He scarcely touched her, but you never know where you are with any horse. That mare, which had been a mirror of all the virtues all the afternoon, was off like a rocket. She overtook an electric car as if it had been standing still. Ellis sawed her mouth; he might as well have sawed the funnel of a locomotive. He had meant to turn off and traverse Bursley by secluded streets, but he perceived that safety lay solely in letting her go straight ahead up the very steep slope of Oldcastle Street into the middle of the town. It would be an amazing mare that galloped to the top of Oldcastle Street! She galloped nearly to the top, and then Ellis began to get hold of her a bit.

'Don't be afraid,' he said masculinely to Ada.

And, conscious of victory, he jerked the mare to the left to avoid an approaching car....

The next instant they were anchored against the roots of a lamp-post. When Ellis saw the upper half of the lamp-post bent down at right angles, and pieces of glass covering the pavement, he could not believe that he and his dogcart had done that, especially as neither the mare, nor the dogcart, nor its freight, was damaged. The machine was merely jammed, and the mare, satisfied, stood quiet, breathing rapidly.

But Ada Jenkins was crying.

And the car stopped a moment to observe. And then a number of chapel-goers on their way to the Sytch Chapel, which the Carter family still faithfully attended, joined the scene; and then a policeman.

Ellis sat like a stuck pig in the dogcart. He knew that speech was demanded of him, but he did not know where to begin.

The worst thing of all was the lamp-post, bent, moveless, unnatural, atrociously comic, accusing him.

The affair was over the town in a minute; the next morning it reached Llandudno. Ellis Carter had been out on the spree with *a Wakes girl* in a dogcart on Sunday afternoon, and had got into such a condition that he had driven into a lamp-post at the top of Oldcastle Street just as people were going into chapel.

The lamp-post remained bent for three days—a fearful warning to all dogs that doggishness has limits.

If it had not been a dogcart, and such a high, green dogcart; if it had been, say, a brougham, or even a cab! If it had not been Sunday! And, granting Sunday, if it had not been just as people were going into chapel! If he had not chosen that particular lamp-post, visible both from the market-place and St. Luke's Square! If he had only contrived to destroy a less obtrusive lamp-post in some unfrequented street! And if it had not been a Wakes girl—if the reprobate had only selected for his guilty amours an actress from one of the touring companies, or even a star from the Hanbridge Empire—yea, or even a local barmaid! But *a Wakes girl!*

Ellis himself saw the enormity of his transgression. He lay awake astounded by his own doggishness.

And yet he had seldom felt less doggy than during that trip. It seemed to him that doggishness was not the glorious thing he had thought. However, he cut a heroic figure at the dogs' club. Every admiring face said: 'Well, you *have* been going the pace! We always knew you were a hot un, but, really——'

V

On the following Friday evening, when Ellis jumped off the car opposite his home on the Hawkins, he saw in the road, halted, a train of vast and queer-shaped waggons in charge of two traction-engines. They were painted on all sides with the great name of Jenkins. They contained Jenkins's roundabouts and shooting-saloons, on their way to rouse the joy of life in other towns. And he perceived in front of the portico the high, green dogcart and the lamp-post-destroying mare.

He went in. The family had come home that afternoon. Sundry of his sisters greeted him with silent horror on their faces in the hall. In the breakfast-room, which gave off the drawing-room, was his mother in the attitude of an intent listener. She spoke no word.

And Ellis listened, too.

'Yes,' a very powerful and raucous voice was saying in the drawing-room, 'I reckoned I'd call and tell ye myself, Mister Carter, what I thought on it. My gell, a motherless gell, but brought up respectable; sixth standard at Whalley Range Board School; and her aunt a strict God-fearing woman! And here your son comes along and gets hold of the girl while her aunt's at the special service for Wakes folks in Bethesda Chapel, and runs off with her in my dogcart with one of my hosses, and raises a scandal all o'er the Five Towns. God bless my soul, mister! I tell'n ye I hardly liked to open o' Monday afternoon, I was that ashamed! And I packed Ada off to Manchester. It seems to me that if the upper classes, as they call 'em—the immoral classes *I* call 'em—'ud look after themselves a bit instead o' looking after other people so much, things might be a bit better, Mister Carter. I dare say you think it's nothing as your son should go about ruining the reputation of any decent, respectable girl as he happens to fancy, Mister Carter; but this is what I say. I say——'

Mr. Carter was understood to assert, in his most pacific and pained public-meeting voice, that he regretted, infinitely regretted——

Mrs. Carter, weeping, ran out of the breakfast-room.

And soon afterwards the traction-engines rumbled off, and the high, green dogcart followed them.

Ellis sat spell-bound.

He heard the parlourmaid go into the drawing-room and announce, 'Tea is ready, sir!' and then his father's dry cough.

And then the parlourmaid came into the breakfast-room: 'Tea is ready, Mr. Ellis!'

Oh, the meal!

A FEUD

When Clive Timmis paused at the side-door of Ezra Brunt's great shop in Machin Street, and the door was opened to him by Ezra Brunt's daughter before he had had time to pull the bell, not only all Machin Street knew it within the hour, but also most persons of consequence left in Hanbridge on a Thursday afternoon—Thursday being early-closing day. For Hanbridge, though it counts sixty thousand inhabitants, and is the chief of the Five Towns—that vast, huddled congeries of boroughs devoted to the manufacture of earthenware—is a place where the art of attending to other people's business still flourishes in rustic perfection.

Ezra Brunt's drapery establishment was the foremost retail house, in any branch of trade, of the Five Towns. It had no rival nearer than Manchester, thirty-six miles off; and even Manchester could exhibit nothing conspicuously superior to it. The most acutely critical shoppers of the Five Towns—women who were in the habit of going to London every year for the January sales—spoke of Brunt's as a 'right-down good shop.' And the husbands of these ladies, manufacturers who employed from two hundred to a thousand men, regarded Ezra Brunt as a commercial magnate of equal importance with themselves. Brunt, who had served his apprenticeship at Birmingham, started business in Machin Street in 1862, when Hanbridge was half its present size and all the best shops of the district were in Oldcastle, an ancient burg contiguous with, but holding itself proudly aloof from, the industrial Five Towns. He paid eighty pounds a year rent, and lived over the shop, and in the summer quarter his gas bill was always under a sovereign. For ten years success tarried, but in 1872 his daughter Eva was born and his wife died, and from that moment the sun of his prosperity climbed higher and higher into heaven. He had been profoundly attached to his wife, and, having lost her he abandoned himself to the mercantile struggle with that morose and terrible ferocity which was the root of his character. Of rude, gaunt aspect, gruffly taciturn by nature, and variable in temper, he yet had the precious instinct for soothing customers. To this day he can surpass his own shop-walkers in the admirable and tender solicitude with which, forsaking dialect, he drops into a lady's ear his famous stereotyped phrase: 'Are you receiving proper attention, madam?' From the first he eschewed the facile trickeries and ostentations which allure the populace. He sought a high-class trade, and by waiting he found it. He would never advertise on hoardings; for many years he had no signboard over his shop-front; and whereas the name of 'Bostocks,' the huge cheap drapers lower down Machin Street, on the opposite side, attacks you at every railway-station and in every tramcar, the name of 'E. Brunt' is to be seen only in a modest regular advertisement on the front page of the *Staffordshire Signal*. Repose, reticence, respectability—it was these attributes which he decided his shop should possess, and by means of which he succeeded. To enter Brunt's, with its silently swinging doors, its broad, easy staircases, its long floors covered with warm, red linoleum, its partitioned walls, its smooth mahogany counters, its unobtrusive mirrors, its rows of youths and virgins in black, and its pervading atmosphere of quietude and discretion, was like entering a temple before the act of oblation has commenced. You were conscious of some supreme administrative influence everywhere imposing itself. That influence was Ezra Brunt. And yet the man differed utterly from the thing he had created. His was one of those dark and passionate souls which smoulder in this harsh Midland district as slag-heaps smoulder on the pit-banks, revealing their strange fires only in the darkness.

In 1899 Brunt's establishment occupied four shops, Nos. 52, 56, 58, and 60, in Machin Street. He had bought the freeholds at a price which timid people regarded as exorbitant, but the solicitors of Hanbridge secretly applauded his enterprise and shrewdness in anticipating the enormous rise in ground-values which has now been in rapid, steady progress there for more than a decade. He had thrown the interiors together and rebuilt the frontages in handsome freestone. He had also purchased several shops opposite, and rumour said that it was his intention to offer these latter to the Town Council at a low figure if the Council would cut a new street leading from his premises to the Market Square. Such a scheme would have met with general approval. But there was one serious hiatus in the plans of Ezra Brunt—to wit, No. 54, Machin Street. No. 54, separating 52 and 56, was a chemist's shop, shabby but sedate as to appearance, owned and occupied by George Christopher Timmis, a mild and venerable citizen, and a local preacher in the Wesleyan Methodist Connexion. For nearly thirty years Brunt had coveted Mr. Timmis's shop; more than twenty years have elapsed since he first opened negotiations for it. Mr. Timmis was by no means eager to sell—indeed, his attitude was distinctly a repellent one—but a bargain would undoubtedly have been concluded had not a report reached the ears of Mr. Timmis to the effect that Ezra Brunt had remarked at the Turk's Head that 'th' old leech was only sticking out for every brass farthing he could get.' The report was untrue, but Mr. Timmis believed it, and from that moment Ezra Brunt's chances of obtaining the chemist's shop vanished completely. His lawyer expended diplomacy in vain, raising the offer week by week till the incredible sum of three thousand pounds was reached. Then Ezra Brunt himself saw Mr. Timmis, and without a word of prelude said:

'Will ye take three thousand guineas for this bit o' property?'

'Not thirty thousand guineas,' said Mr. Timmis quietly; the stern pride of the benevolent old local preacher had been aroused.

'Then be damned to you!' said Ezra Brunt, who had never been known to swear before.

Thenceforth a feud existed, not less bitter because it was a feud in which nothing was said and nothing done—a silent and implacable mutual resistance. The sole outward sign of it was the dirty and stumpy brown-brick shop-front of Mr. Timmis, squeezed in between those massive luxurious façades of stone which Ezra Brunt soon afterwards erected. The pharmaceutical business of Mr. Timmis was not a very large one, and, fiscally, Ezra Brunt could have swallowed him at a meal and suffered no inconvenience; but in that the aged chemist had lived on just half his small income for some fifty years past, his position was impregnable. Hanbridge smiled cynically at this *impasse* produced by an idle word, and, recognising the equality of the antagonists, leaned neither to one side nor to the other. At intervals, however, the legend of the feud was embroidered with new and effective detail in the mouth of some inventive gossip, and by degrees it took high place among those piquant social histories which illustrate the real life of a town, and which parents recount to their children with such zest in moods of reminiscence.

When George Christopher Timmis buried his wife, Ezra Brunt, as a near neighbour, was asked to the funeral. 'The cortège will move at 1.30,' ran the printed invitation, and at 1.15 Brunt's carriage was decorously in place behind the hearse and the two mourning-coaches. The demeanour of the chemist and the draper towards each other was a sublime answer to the demands of the occasion; some people even said that the breach had been healed, but these were not of the discerning.

The most active person at the funeral was the chemist's only nephew, Clive Timmis, partner in a small but prosperous firm of majolica manufacturers at Bursley. Clive, who was seldom seen in Hanbridge, made a favourable impression on everyone by his pleasing, unaffected manner and his air of discretion and success. He was a bachelor of thirty-two, and lived in lodgings at Bursley. On the return of the funeral-party from the cemetery, Clive Timmis found Brunt's daughter Eva in his uncle's house. Uninvited, she had left her place in the private room at her father's shop in order to assist Timmis's servant Sarah in the preparation of that solid and solemn repast which must inevitably follow every proper interment in the Five Towns. Without false modesty, she introduced herself to one or two of the men who had surprised her at her work, and then quietly departed just as they were sitting down to table and Sarah had brought in the hot tea-cakes. Clive Timmis saw her only for a moment, but from that moment she was his one thought. During the evening, which he spent alone with his uncle, he behaved in every particular as a nephew should, yet he was acting a part; his real self roved after Ezra Brunt's daughter, wherever she might be. Clive had never fallen in love, though several times in his life he had tried hard to do so. He had long wished to marry—wished ardently; he had even got into the way of regarding every woman he met—and he met many—in the light of a possible partner. 'Can it be *she?* he had asked himself a thousand times, and then answered half sadly, 'No.' Not one woman had touched his imagination, coincided with his dream. It is strange that after seeing Eva Brunt he forgot thus to interrogate himself. For a fortnight, while he went his ways as usual, her image occupied his heart, throwing that once orderly chamber into the wildest confusion; and he let it remain, dimly aware of some delicious danger. He inspected the image every night before he slept, and every morning when he awoke, and made no effort to define its distracting charm; he knew only that Eva Brunt was absolutely and in every detail unlike all other women. On the second Sunday he murmured during the sermon: 'But I only saw her for a minute.' A few days afterwards he took the tram to Hanbridge.

'Uncle,' he said, 'how should you like me to come and live here with you? I've been thinking things out a bit, and I thought perhaps you'd like it. I expect you must feel rather lonely now.'

The neat, fragrant shop was empty, and the two men stood behind the big glass-fronted case of Burroughs and Wellcome's preparations. Clive's venerable uncle happened to be looking into a drawer marked 'Gentianæ Rad. Pulv.' He closed the drawer with slow hesitation, and then, stroking his long white beard, replied in that deliberate voice which seemed always to tremble with religious fervour:

'The hand of the Lord is in this thing, Clive. I have wished that you might come to live here with me. But I was afraid it would be too far from the works.'

'Pooh! that's nothing,' said Clive.

As he lingered at the shop door for the Bursley car to pass the end of Machin Street, Eva Brunt went by. He raised his hat with diffidence, and she smiled. It was a marvellous chance. His heart leapt into a throb which was half agony and half delight.

'I am in love,' he said gravely.

He had just discovered the fact, and the discovery filled him with exquisite apprehension.

If he had waited till the age of thirty-two for that springtime of the soul which we call love, Clive had not waited for nothing. Eva was a woman to enravish the heart of a man whose imagination could pierce the agitating secrets immured in that calm and silent bosom. Slender and scarcely tall, she belonged to the order of spare, slight-made women, who hide within their slim frames an endowment of profound passion far exceeding that of their more voluptuously-formed sisters, who never coarsen into stoutness, and who at forty are as disturbing as at twenty. At this date Eva was twenty-six. She had a rather small, white face, which was a mask to the casual observer, and the very mirror of her feelings to anyone with eyes to read its signs.

'I tell you what you are like,' said Clive to her once: 'you are like a fine racehorse, always on the quiver.'

Yet many people considered her cold and impassive. Her walk and bearing showed a sensitive independence, and when she spoke it was usually in tones of command. The girls in the shop, where she was a power second only to Ezra Brunt, were a little afraid of her, chiefly because she poured terrible scorn on their small affectations, jealousies, and vendettas. But they liked her because, in their own phrase, 'there was no nonsense about' this redoubtable woman. She hated shams and make-believes with a bitter and ruthless hatred. She was the heiress to at least five thousand a year, and knew it well, but she never encouraged her father to complicate their simple mode of life with the pomps of wealth. They lived in a house with a large garden at Pireford, which is on the summit of the steep ridge between the Five Towns and Oldcastle, and they kept two servants and a coachman, who was also gardener. Eva paid the servants good wages, and took care to get good value therefor.

'It's not often I have any bother with my servants,' she would say, 'for they know that if there is any trouble I would just as soon clear them out and put on an apron and do the work myself.'

She was an accomplished house-mistress, and could bake her own bread: in towns not one woman in a thousand can bake. With the coachman she had little to do, for she could not rid herself of a sentimental objection to the carriage—it savoured of 'airs'; when she used it she used it as she might use a tramcar. It was her custom, every day except Saturday, to walk to the shop about eleven o'clock, after her house had been set in order. She had been thoroughly trained in the business, and had spent a year at a first-rate shop in High Street, Kensington. Millinery was her speciality, and she still watched over that department with a particular attention; but for some time past she had risen beyond the limitations of departments, and assisted her father in the general management of the vast concern. In commercial aptitude she resembled the typical Frenchwoman.

Although he was her father, Ezra Brunt had the wit to recognise her talents, and he always listened to her suggestions, which, however, sometimes startled him. One of them was that he should import into the Five Towns a modiste from Paris, offering a salary of two hundred a year. The old provincial stood aghast. He had the idea that all Parisian women were stage-dancers. And to pay four pounds a week to a female!

Nevertheless, Mademoiselle Bertot—styled in the shop 'Madame'—now presides over Ezra Brunt's dressmakers, draws her four pounds a week (of which she saves two), and by mere nationality has given a unique distinction and success to her branch of the business.

Eva occupied a small room opening off the principal showroom, and during hours of work she issued thence but seldom. Only customers of the highest importance might speak with her. She was a power felt rather than seen. Employés who knocked at her door always did so with a certain awe of what awaited them on the other side, and a consciousness that the moment was unsuitable for levity. 'If you please, Miss Eva——'. Here she gave audience to the 'buyers' and window-dressers, listened to complaints and excuses, and occasionally had a secret orgy of afternoon tea with one or two of her friends. None but these few girls—mostly younger than herself, and remarkable only in that their dislike of the snobbery of the Five Towns, though less fiercely displayed, agreed with her own—really knew Eva. To them alone did she unveil herself, and by them she was idolized.

'She is simply splendid when you know her—such a jolly girl!' they would say to other people; but other people, especially other women, could not believe it. They fearfully respected her because she was very well dressed and had quantities of money. But they called her 'a curious creature'; it was inconceivable to them that she should choose to work in a shop; and her tongue had a causticity which was sometimes exceedingly disconcerting and mortifying. As for men, she was shy of them, and, moreover, she loathed the elaborate and insincere ritual of deference which the average man practises towards women unrelated to him, particularly when they are young and rich. Her father she adored, without knowing it; for he often angered her, and humiliated her in private. As for the rest, she was, after all, only six-and-twenty.

'If you don't mind, I should like to walk along with you,' Clive Timmis said to her one Sunday evening in the porch of the Bethesda Chapel.

'I shall be glad,' she answered at once; 'father isn't here, and I'm all alone.'

Ezra Brunt was indeed seldom there, counting in the matter of attendance at chapel among what were called 'the weaker brethren.'

'I am going over to Oldcastle,' Clive explained calmly.

So began the formal courtship—more than a month after Clive had settled in Machin Street, for he was far too discreet to engender by precipitancy any suspicion in the haunts of scandal that his true reason for establishing himself in his uncle's household was a certain rich young woman who was to be found every day next door. Guided as much by instinct as by tact, Clive approached Eva with an almost savage simplicity and naturalness of manner, ignoring not only her father's wealth, but all the feigned punctilio of a wooer. His face said: 'Let there be no beating about the bush—I like you.' Hers answered: 'Good! we will see.'

From the first he pleased her, and not least in treating her exactly as she would have wished to be treated—namely, as a quite plain person of that part of the middle class which is neither upper nor lower. Few men in the Five Towns would have been capable of forgetting Ezra Brunt's income in talking to Ezra Brunt's daughter. Fortunately, Timmis had a proud, confident spirit—the spirit of one who, unaided, has wrested success from the world's deathlike clutch. Had Eva the reversion of fifty thousand a year instead of five, he, Clive, was still a prosperous plain man, well able to support a wife in the position to which God had called him.

Their walks together grew more and more frequent, and they became intimate, exchanging ideas and rejoicing openly at the similarity of those ideas. Although there was no concealment in these encounters, still, there was a circumspection which resembled the clandestine. By a silent understanding Clive did not enter the house at Pireford; to have done so would have excited remark, for this house, unlike some, had never been the rendezvous of young men; much less, therefore, did he invade the shop. No! The chief part of their love-making (for such it was, though the term would have roused Eva's contemptuous anger) occurred in the streets; in this they did but follow the traditions of their class. Thus, the idyll, so matter-of-fact upon the surface, but within which glowed secret and adorable fires, progressed towards its culmination. Eva, the artless fool—oh, how simple are the wisest at times!—thought that the affair was hid from the shop. But was it possible? Was it possible that in those tiny bedrooms on the third floor, where the heavy evening hours were ever lightened with breathless interminable recitals of what some 'he' had said and some 'she' had replied, such an enthralling episode should escape discovery? The dormitories knew of Eva's 'attachment' before Eva herself. Yet none knew how it was known. The whisper arose like Venus from a sea of trivial gossip, miraculously, exquisitely. On the night when the first rumour of it traversed the passages there was scarcely any sleep at Brunt's, while Eva up at Pireford slumbered as a young girl.

On the Thursday afternoon with which we began, Brunt's was deserted save for the housekeeper and Eva, who was writing letters in her room.

'I saw you from my window, coming up the street,' she said to Clive, 'and so I ran down to open the door. Will you come into father's room? He is in Manchester for the day, buying.

'I knew that,' said Timmis.

'How did you know?' She observed that his manner was somewhat nervous and constrained.

'You yourself told me last night—don't you remember?'

'So I did.'

'That's why I sent the note round this morning to say I'd call this afternoon. You got it, I suppose?'

She nodded thoughtfully.

'Well, what is this business you want to talk about?'

It was spoken with a brave carelessness, but he caught the tremor in her voice, and saw her little hand shake as it lay on the table amid her father's papers. Without knowing why he should do so, he stepped hastily forward and seized that hand. Her emotion unmanned him. He thought he was going to cry; he could not account for himself.

'Eva,' he said thickly, 'you know what the business is; you know, don't you?'

She smiled. That smile, the softness of her hand, the sparkle in her eye, the heave of her small bosom ... it was the divinest miracle! Clive, manufacturer of majolica, went hot and then cold, and then his wits were suddenly his own again.

'That's all right,' he murmured, and sighed, and placed on Eva's lips the first kiss that had ever lain there.

'Dear boy,' she said later, 'you should have come up to Pireford, not here, and when father was there.'

'Should I?' he answered happily. 'It just occurred to me all of a sudden this morning that you would be here, and that I couldn't wait.'

'You will come up to-night and see father?'

'I had meant to.'

'You had better go home now.'

'Had I?'

She nodded, putting her lips tightly together—a trick of hers.

'Come up about half-past eight.'

'Good! I will let myself out.'

He left her, and she gazed dreamily at the window, which looked on to a whitewashed yard. The next moment someone else entered the room with heavy footsteps. She turned round a little startled.

It was her father.

'Why! You *are* back early, father! How——' She stopped. Something in the old man's glance gave her a premonition of disaster. To this day she does not know what accident brought him from Manchester two hours sooner than usual, and to Machin Street instead of Pireford.

'Has young Timmis been here?' he inquired curtly.

'Yes.'

'Ha!' with subdued, sinister satisfaction, 'I saw him going out. He didna see me.' Ezra Brunt deposited his hat and sat down.

Intimate with all her father's various moods, she saw instantly and with terrible certainty that a series of chances had fatally combined themselves against her. If only she had not happened to tell Clive that her father would be at Manchester this day! If only her father had adhered to his customary hour of return! If only Clive had had the sense to make his proposal openly at Pireford some evening! If only he had left a little earlier! If only her father had not caught him going out by the side-door on a Thursday afternoon when the place was empty! Here, she guessed, was the suggestion of furtiveness which had raised her father's unreasoning anger, often fierce, and always incalculable.

'Clive Timmis has asked me to marry him, father.'

'Has he!'

'Surely you must have known, father, that he and I were seeing each other a great deal.'

'Not from your lips, my girl.'

'Well, father——' Again she stopped, this strong and capable woman, gifted with a fine brain to organize and a powerful will to command. She quailed, robbed of speech, before the causeless, vindictive, and infantile wrath of an old man who happened to be in a bad temper. She actually felt like a naughty schoolgirl before him. Such is the tremendous influence of lifelong habit, the irresistible power of the *patria potestas* when it has never been relaxed. Ezra Brunt saw in front of him only a cowering child. 'Clive is coming up to see you to-night,' she went on timidly, clearing her throat.

'Humph! Is he?'

The rosy and tender dream of five minutes ago lay in fragments at Eva's feet. She brooded with stricken apprehension upon the forms of obstruction which his despotism might choose.

The next morning Clive and his uncle breakfasted together as usual in the parlour behind, the chemist's shop.

'Uncle,' said Clive brusquely, when the meal was nearly finished, 'I'd better tell you that I've proposed to Eva Brunt.'

Old George Timmis lowered the *Manchester Guardian* and gazed at Clive over his steel-rimmed spectacles.

'She is a good girl,' he remarked; 'she will make you a good wife. Have you spoken to her father?'

'That's the point. I saw him last night, and I'll tell you what he said. These were his words: "You can marry my daughter, Mr. Timmis, when your uncle agrees to part with his shop!"'

'That I shall never do, nephew,' said the aged patriarch quietly and deliberately.

'Of course you won't, uncle. I shouldn't think of suggesting it. I'm merely telling you what he said.' Clive laughed harshly. 'Why,' he added, 'the man must be mad!'

'What did the young woman say to that?' his uncle inquired.

Clive frowned.

'I didn't see her last night,' he said. 'I didn't ask to see her. I was too angry.'

Just then the post arrived, and there was a letter for Clive, which he read and put carefully in his waistcoat pocket.

'Eva writes asking me to go to Pireford to-night,' he said, after a pause. 'I'll soon settle it, depend on that. If Ezra Brunt refuses his consent, so much the worse for him. I wonder whether he actually imagines that a grown man and a grown woman are to be.... Ah well, I can't talk about it! It's too silly. I'll be off to the works.'

When Clive reached Pireford that night, Eva herself opened the door to him. She was wearing a gray frock, and over it a large white apron, perfectly plain.

'My girls are both out to-night,' she said, 'and I was making some puffs for the sewing-meeting tea. Come into the breakfast-room.... This way,' she added, guiding him. He had entered the house on the previous night for the first time. She spoke hurriedly, and, instead of stopping in the breakfast-room, wandered uncertainly through it into the greenhouse, to which it gave access by means of a French window. In the dark, confined space, amid the close-packed blossoms, they stood together. She bent down to smell at a musk-plant. He took her hand and drew her soft and yielding form towards him and kissed her warm face.

'Oh, Clive!' she said. 'Whatever are we to do?'

'Do?' he replied, enchanted by her instinctive feminine surrender and reliance upon him, which seemed the more precious in that creature so proud and reserved to all others. 'Do! Where is your father?'

'Reading the *Signal* in the dining-room.'

Every business man in the Five Towns reads the *Staffordshire Signal* from beginning to end every night.

'I will see him. Of course he is your father; but I will just tell him—as decently as I can—that neither you nor I will stand this nonsense.'

'You mustn't—you mustn't see him.'

'Why not?'

'It will only lead to unpleasantness.'

'That can't be helped.'

'He never, never changes when once he has *said* a thing. I know him.'

Clive was arrested by something in her tone, something new to him, that in its poignant finality seemed to have caught up and expressed in a single instant that bitterness of a lifetime's renunciation which falls to the lot of most women.

'Will you come outside?' he asked in a different voice.

Without replying, she led the way down the long garden, which ended in an ivy-grown brick wall and a panorama of the immense valley of industries below. It was a warm, cloudy evening. The last silver tinge of an August twilight lay on the shoulder of the hill to the left. There was no moon, but the splendid watch-fires of labour flamed from ore-heap and furnace across the whole expanse, performing their nightly miracle of beauty. Trains crept with noiseless mystery along the middle distance, under their canopies of yellow steam. Further off the far-extending streets of Hanbridge made a map of starry lines on the blackness. To the south-east stared the cold, blue electric lights of Knype railway-station. All was silent, save for a distant thunderous roar, the giant breathing of the forge at Cauldon Bar Ironworks.

Eva leaned both elbows on the wall and looked forth.

'Do you mean to say,' said Clive, 'that Mr. Brunt will actually stick by what he has said?'

'Like grim death,' said Eva.

'But what's his idea?'

'Oh! how can I tell you?' she burst out passionately.

'Perhaps I did wrong. Perhaps I ought to have warned him earlier—said to him, "Father, Clive Timmis is courting me!" Ugh! He cannot bear to be surprised about anything. But yet he must have known.... It was all an accident, Clive—all an accident. He saw you leaving the shop yesterday. He would say he *caught* you leaving the shop—*sneaking* off like——'

'But, Eva——'

'I know—I know! Don't tell me! But it was that, I am sure. He would resent the mere look of things, and then he would think and think, and the notion of your uncle's shop would occur to him again, after all these years. I can see his thoughts as plain ... My dear, if he had not seen you at Machin Street yesterday, or if you had seen him and spoken to him, all might have gone right. He would have objected, but he would have given way in a day or two. Now he will never give way! I asked you just now what was to be done, but I knew all the time that there was nothing.'

'There is one thing to be done, Eva, and the sooner the better.'

'Do you mean that old Mr. Timmis must give up his shop to my father? Never! never!'

'I mean,' said Clive quietly, 'that we must marry without your father's consent.'

She shook her head slowly and sadly, relapsing into calmness.

'You shake your head, Eva, but it must be so.'

'I can't, my dear.'

'Do you mean to say that you will allow your father's childish whim—for it's nothing else; he can't find any objection to me as a husband for you, and he knows it—that you will allow his childish whim to spoil your life and mine? Remember, you are twenty-six and I am thirty-two.'

'I can't do it! I daren't! I'm mad with myself for feeling like this, but I daren't! And even if I dared I wouldn't. Clive, you don't know! You can't tell how it is!'

Her sorrowful, pathetic firmness daunted him. She was now composed, mistress again of herself, and her moral force dominated him.

'Then, you and I are to be unhappy all our lives, Eva?'

The soft influences of the night seemed to direct her voice as, after a long pause, she uttered the words: 'No one is ever quite unhappy in all this world.'

There was another pause, as she gazed steadily down into the wonderful valley. 'We must wait.'

'Wait!' echoed Clive with angry grimness. 'He will live for twenty years!'

'No one is ever quite unhappy in all this world,' she repeated dreamily, as one might turn over a treasure in order to examine it.

Now for the epilogue to the feud. Two years passed, and it happened that there was to be a Revival at the Bethesda Chapel. One morning the superintendent minister and the revivalist called on Ezra Brunt at his shop. When informed of their presence, the great draper had an impulse of anger, for, like many stouter chapel-goers than himself, he would scarcely tolerate the intrusion of religion into commerce. However, the visit had an air of ceremony, and he could not decline to see these ambassadors of heaven in his private room. The revivalist, a cheery, shrewd man, whose powers of organization were obvious, and who seemed to put organization before everything else, pleased Ezra Brunt at once.

'We want a specially good congregation at the opening meeting to-night,' said the revivalist. 'Now, the basis of a good congregation must necessarily be the regular pillars of the church, and therefore we are making a few calls this morning to insure the presence of our chief men—the men of influence and position. You will come, Mr. Brunt, and you will let it be known among your employés that they will please you by coming too?'

Ezra Brunt was by no means a regular pillar of the Bethesda, but he had a vague sensation of flattery, and he consented; indeed, there was no alternative.

The first hymn was being sung when he reached the chapel. To his surprise, he found the place crowded in every part. A man whom he did not know led him to a wooden form which had been put in the space between the front pews and the Communion-rail. He felt strange there, and uneasy, apprehensive.

The usual discreet somnolence of the chapel had been disturbed as by some indecorous but formidable awakener; the air was electric; anything might occur. Ezra was astounded by the mere volume of the singing; never had he heard such singing. At the end of the hymn the congregation sat down, hiding their faces in expectation. The revivalist stood erect and terrible in the pulpit, no longer a shrewd, cheery man of the world, but the very mouthpiece of the wrath and mercy of God. Ezra's self-importance dwindled before that gaze, till, from a renowned magnate of the Five Towns, he became an item in the multitude of suppliants. He profoundly wished he had never come.

'Remember the hymn,' said the revivalist, with austere emphasis:

**'"My richest gain I count but loss,
And pour contempt on all my pride."'**

The admirable histrionic art with which he intensified the consonants in the last line produced a tremendous effect. Not for nothing was this man cerebrated throughout Methodism as a saver of souls. When, after a pause, he raised his hand and ejaculated, 'Let us pray,' sobs could be heard throughout the chapel. The Revival had begun.

At the end of a quarter of an hour Ezra Brunt would have given fifty pounds to be outside, but he could not stir; he was magnetized. Soon the revivalist came down from the pulpit and stood within the Communion-rail, whence he addressed the nearmost part of the people in low, soothing tones of persuasion. Apparently he ignored Ezra Brunt, but the man was convicted of sin, and felt himself melting like an icicle in front of a fire. He recalled the days of his youth, the piety of his father and mother, and the long traditions of a stern Dissenting family. He had backslidden, slackened in the use of the means of grace, run after the things of this world. It is true that none of his chiefest iniquities presented themselves to him; he was quite unconscious of them even then; but the lesser ones were more than sufficient to overwhelm him. Class-leaders were now reasoning with stricken sinners, and Ezra, who could not take his eyes off the revivalist, heard the footsteps of those who were going to the 'inquiry-room' for more private counsel. In vain he argued that he was about to be ridiculous; that the idea of him, Ezra Brunt, a professed Wesleyan for half a century, being publicly 'saved' at the age of fifty-seven was not to be entertained; that the town would talk; that his business might suffer if for any reason he should be morally bound to apply to it too strictly the principles of the New Testament. He was under the spell. The tears coursed down his long cheeks, and he forgot to care, but sat entranced by the revivalist's marvellous voice. Suddenly, with an awful sob, he bent and hid his face in his hands. The spectacle of the old, proud man helpless in the grasp of profound emotion was a sight to rend the heart-strings.

'Brother, be of good cheer,' said a tremulous and benign voice above him. 'The love of God compasseth all things. Only believe.'

He looked up and saw the venerable face and long white beard of George Christopher Timmis.

Ezra Brunt shrank away, embittered and ashamed.

'I cannot,' he murmured with difficulty.

'The love of God is all-powerful.'

'Will it make you part with that bit o' property, think you?' said Ezra Brunt, with a kind of despairing ferocity.

'Brother,' replied the aged servant of God, unmoved, 'if my shop is in truth a stumbling-block in this solemn hour, you shall have it.'

Ezra Brunt was staggered.

'I believe! I believe!' he cried.

'Praise God!' said the chemist, with majestic joy.

Three months afterwards Eva Brunt and Clive Timmis were married. It is characteristic of the fine sentimentality which underlies the surface harshness of the inhabitants of the Five Towns that, though No. 54 Machin Street was duly transferred to Ezra Brunt, the chemist retiring from business, he has never rebuilt it to accord with the rest of his premises. In all its shabbiness it stands between the other big dazzling shops as a reminding monument.

PHANTOM

I

The heart of the Five Towns—that undulating patch of England covered with mean streets, and dominated by tall smoking chimneys, whence are derived your cups and saucers and plates, some of your coal, and a portion of your iron—is Hanbridge, a borough larger and busier than its four sisters, and even more grimy and commonplace than they. And the heart of Hanbridge is probably the offices of the Five Towns Banking Company, where the last trace of magic and romance is beaten out of human existence, and the meaning of life is expressed in balances, deposits, percentages, and overdrafts—especially overdrafts. In a fine suite of rooms on the first floor of the bank building resides Mr. Lionel Woolley, the manager, with his wife May and their children. Mrs. Woolley is compelled to change her white window-curtains once a week because of the smuts. Mr. Woolley, forty-five, rather bald, frigidly suave, positive, egotistic, and pontifical, is a specimen of the man of business who is nothing else but a man of business. His career has been a calculation from which sentiment is entirely omitted; he has no instinct for the things which cannot be defined and assessed. Scarcely a manufacturer in Hanbridge but who inimically and fearfully regards Mr. Woolley as an amazing instance of a creature without a soul; and the absence of soul in a fellow-man must be very marked indeed before a Hanbridge manufacturer notices it. There are some sixty thousand immortal souls in Hanbridge, but they seldom attract attention.

Yet Mr. Woolley was once brought into contact with the things which cannot be defined and assessed; once he stood face to face with some strange visible resultant of those secret forces that lie beyond the human ken. And, moreover, the adventure affected the whole of his domestic life. The wonder and the pathos of the story lie in the fact that Nature, prodigal though she is known to be, should have wasted the rare and beautiful visitation on just Mr. Woolley. Mr. Woolley was bathed in romance of the most singular kind, and the precious fluid ran off him like water off a duck's back.

II

Ten years ago on a Thursday afternoon in July, Lionel Woolley, as he walked up through the new park at Bursley to his celibate rooms in Park Terrace, was making addition sums out of various items connected with the institution of marriage. Bursley is next door to Hanbridge, and Lionel happened then to be cashier of the Bursley branch of the bank. He had in mind two possible wives, each of whom possessed advantages which appealed to him, and he was unable to decide between them by any mathematical process. Suddenly, from a glazed shelter near the empty bandstand, there emerged in front of him one of the delectable creatures who had excited his fancy. May Lawton was twenty-eight, an orphan, and a schoolmistress. She, too, had celibate rooms in Park Terrace, and it was owing to this coincidence that Lionel had made her acquaintance six months previously. She was not pretty, but she was tall, straight, well dressed, well educated, and not lacking in experience; and she had a little money of her own.

'Well, Mr. Woolley,' she said easily, stopping for him as she raised her sunshade, 'how satisfied you look!'

'It's the sight of you,' he replied, without a moment's hesitation.

He had a fine assured way with women (he need not have envied a curate accustomed to sewing meetings), and May Lawton belonged to the type of girl whose demeanour always challenges the masculine in a man. Gazing at her, Lionel was swiftly conscious of several things: the piquancy of her snub nose, the brightness of her smile, at once defiant and wistful, the lingering softness of her gloved hand, and the extraordinary charm of her sunshade, which matched her dress and formed a sort of canopy and frame for that intelligent, tantalizing face. He remembered that of late he and she had grown very intimate; and it came upon him with a shock, as though he had just opened a telegram which said so, that May, and not the other girl, was his destined mate. And he thought of her fortune, tiny but nevertheless useful, and how clever she was, and how inexplicably different from the rest of her sex, and how she would adorn his house, and set him off, and help him in his career. He heard himself saying negligently to friends: 'My wife speaks French like a native. Of course, my wife has travelled a great deal. My wife has thoroughly studied the management of children. Now, my wife does understand the art of dress. I put my wife's bit of money into so-and-so.' In short, Lionel was as near being in love as his character permitted.

And while he walked by May's side past the bowling-greens at the summit of the hill, she lightly quizzing the raw newness of the park and its appurtenances, he wondered, he honestly wondered, that he could ever have hesitated between May Lawton and the other. Her superiority was too obvious; she was a woman of the world! She.... In a flash he knew that he would propose to her that very afternoon. And when he had suggested a stroll towards Moorthorne, and she had deliciously agreed, he was conscious of a tumultuous uplifting and splendid carelessness of spirits. 'Imagine me bringing it to a climax to-day,' he reflected, profoundly pleased with himself. 'Ah well, it will be settled once for all!' He admired his own decision; he was quite struck by it. 'I shall call her May before I leave her,' he thought, gazing at her, and discovering how well the name suited her, with its significances of alertness, geniality, and half-mocking coyness.

'So school is closed,' he said, and added humorously: '"Broken up" is the technical term, I believe.'

'Yes,' she answered, 'and I had walked out into the park to meditate seriously upon the question of my holiday.'

She caught his eye in a net of bright glances, and romance was in the air. They had crossed a couple of smoke-soiled fields, and struck into the old Hanbridge road just below the abandoned toll-house with its broad eaves.

'And whither do your meditations point?' he demanded playfully.

'My meditations point to Switzerland,' she said. 'I have friends in Lausanne.'

The reference to foreign climes impressed him.

'Would that I could go to Switzerland too!' he exclaimed; and privately: 'Now for it! I'm about to begin.'

'Why?' she questioned, with elaborate simplicity.

At the moment, as they were passing the toll-house, the other girl appeared surprisingly from round the corner of the toll-house, where the lane from Toft End joins the highroad. This second creature was smaller than Miss Lawton, less assertive, less intelligent, perhaps, but much more beautiful.

Everyone halted and everyone blushed.

'May!' the interrupter at length stammered.

'May!' responded Miss Lawton lamely.

The other girl was named May too—May Deane, child of the well-known majolica manufacturer, who lived with his sons and daughter in a solitary and ancient house at Toft End.

Lionel Woolley said nothing until they had all shaken hands—his famous way with women seemed to have deserted him—and then he actually stated that he had forgotten an appointment, and must depart. He had gone before the girls could move.

When they were alone, the two Mays fronted each other, confused, hostile, almost homicidal.

'I hope I didn't spoil a *tête-à-tête*,' said May Deane, stiffly and sharply, in a manner quite foreign to her soft and yielding nature.

The schoolmistress, abandoning herself to an inexplicable but overwhelming impulse, took breath for a proud lie.

'No,' she answered; 'but if you had come three minutes earlier——'

She smiled calmly.

'Oh!' murmured May Deane, after a pause.

III

That evening May Deane returned home at half-past nine. She had been with her two brothers to a lawn-tennis party at Hillport, and she told her father, who was reading the *Staffordshire Signal* in his accustomed solitude, that the boys were staying later for cards, but that she had declined to stay because she felt tired. She kissed the old widower good-night, and said that she should go to bed at once. But before retiring she visited the housekeeper in the kitchen in order to discuss certain household matters: Jim's early breakfast, the proper method of washing Herbert's new flannels (Herbert would be very angry if they were shrunk), and the dog-biscuits for Carlo. These questions settled, she went to her room, drew the blind, lighted some candles, and sat down near the window.

She was twenty-two, and she had about her that strange and charming nunlike mystery which often comes to a woman who lives alone and unguessed-at among male relatives. Her room was her bower. No one, save the servants and herself, ever entered it. Mr. Deane and Jim and Bertie might glance carelessly through the open door in passing along the corridor, but had they chanced in idle curiosity to enter, the room would have struck them as unfamiliar, and they might perhaps have exclaimed with momentary interest, 'So this is May's room!' And some hint that May was more than a daughter and sister—a woman, withdrawn, secret, disturbing, living her own inner life side by side with the household life—might have penetrated their obtuse paternal and fraternal masculinity. Her beautiful face (the nose and mouth were perfect, and at either extremity of the upper lip grew a soft down), her dark hair, her quiet voice and her gentle acquiescence (diversified by occasional outbursts of sarcasm), appealed to them and won them; but they accepted her as something of course, as something which went without saying. They adored her, and did not know that they adored her.

May took off her hat, stuck the pins into it again, and threw it on the bed, whose white and green counterpane hung down nearly to the floor on either side. Then she lay back in the chair, and, pulling away the blind, glanced through the window; the moon, rather dim behind the furnace lights of Red Cow Ironworks, was rising over Moorthorne. May dropped the blind with a wearied gesture, and turned within the room, examining its contents as if she had not seen them before: the wardrobe, the chest of drawers, which was also a dressing-table, the washstand, the dwarf book-case with its store of Edna Lyalls, Elizabeth Gaskells, Thackerays, Charlotte Yonges, Charlotte Brontës, a Thomas Hardy or so, and some old school-books. She looked at the pictures, including a sampler worked by a deceased aunt, at the loud-ticking Swiss clock on the mantelpiece, at the higgledy-piggledy photographs there, at the new Axminster carpet, the piece of linoleum in front of the washstand, and the bad joining of the wallpaper to the left of the door. She missed none of the details which she knew so well, with such long monotonous intimacy, and sighed.

Then she got up from the chair, and, opening a small drawer in the chest of drawers, put her hand familiarly to the back and drew forth a photograph. She carried the photograph to the light of the candles on the mantelpiece, and gazed at it attentively, puckering her brows. It was a portrait of Lionel Woolley. Heaven knows by what subterfuge or lucky accident she had obtained it, for Lionel certainly had not given it to her. She loved Lionel. She had loved him for five years, with a love silent, blind, intense, irrational, and too elemental to be concealed. Everyone knew of May's passion. Many women admired her taste; a few were shocked and puzzled by it. All the men of her acquaintance either pitied or despised her for it. Her father said nothing. Her brothers were less cautious, and summed up their opinion of Lionel in the curt, scornful assertion that he showed a tendency to cheat at tennis. But May would never hear ill of him; he was a god to her, and she could not hide her worship. For more than a year, until lately, she had been almost sure of him, and then came a faint vague rumour concerning Lionel and May Lawton, a rumour which she had refused to take seriously. The encounter of that afternoon, and Miss Lawton's triumphant remark, had dazed her. For seven hours she had existed in a kind of semi-conscious delirium, in which she could perceive nothing but the fatal fact, emerging more clearly every moment from the welter of her thoughts, that she had lost Lionel. Lionel had proposed to May Lawton, and been accepted, just before she surprised them together; and Lionel, with a man's excusable cowardice, had left his betrothed to announce the engagement.

She tore up the photograph, put the fragments in the grate, and set a light to them.

Her father's step sounded on the stairs; he hesitated, and knocked sharply at her door.

'What's burning, May?'

'It's all right, father,' she answered calmly, 'I'm only burning some papers in the fire-grate.'

'Well, see you don't burn the house down.'

He passed on.

Then she found a sheet of notepaper, and wrote on it in pencil, using the mantelpiece for a desk: 'Dear home. Good-night, good-bye.' She cogitated, and wrote further: 'Forgive me.—MAY.'

She put the message in an envelope, and wrote on the envelope 'Jim,' and placed it prominently in front of the clock. But after she had looked at it for a minute, she wrote 'Father' above Jim, and then 'Herbert' below.

There were noises in the hall; the boys had returned earlier than she expected. As they went along the corridor and caught a glimpse of her light under the door, Jim cried gaily: 'Now then, out with that light! A little thing like you ought to be asleep hours since.'

She listened for the bang of their door, and then, very hurriedly, she removed her pink frock and put on an old black one, which was rather tight in the waist. And she donned her hat, securing it carefully with both pins, extinguished the candles, and crept quietly downstairs, and so by the back-door into the garden. Carlo, the retriever, came halfway out of his kennel and greeted her in the moonlight with a yawn. She patted his head and ran stealthily up the garden, through the gate, and up the waste green land towards the crown of the hill.

IV

The top of Toft End is the highest land in the Five Towns, and from it may be clearly seen all the lurid evidences of manufacture which sweep across the borders of the sky on north, east, west, and south. North-eastwards lie the moorlands, and far off Manifold, the 'metropolis of the moorlands,' as it is called. On this night the furnaces of Red Cow Ironworks, in the hollow to the east, were in full blast; their fluctuating yellow light illuminated queerly the grass of the fields above Deane's house, and the regular roar of their breathing reached that solitary spot like the distant rumour of some leviathan beast angrily fuming. Further away to the south-west the Cauldon Bar Ironworks reproduced the same phenomena, and round the whole horizon, near and far, except to the north-east, the lesser fires of labour leapt and flickered and glinted in their mists of smoke, burning ceaselessly, as they burned every night and every day at all seasons of all years. The town of Bursley slept in the deep valley to the west, and vast Hanbridge in the shallower depression to the south, like two sleepers accustomed to rest quietly amid great disturbances; the beacons of their Town Halls and churches kept watch, and the whole scene was dominated by the placidity of the moon, which had now risen clear of the Red Cow furnace clouds, and was passing upwards through tracts of stars.

Into this scene, climbing up from the direction of Manifold, came Lionel Woolley, nearly at midnight, having walked some eighteen miles in a vain effort to re-establish his self-satisfaction by a process of reasoning and ingenious excuses. Lionel felt that in the brief episode of the afternoon he had scarcely behaved with dignity. In other words, he was fully and painfully aware that he must have looked a fool, a coward, an ass, a contemptible and pitiful person, in the eyes of at least one girl, if not of two. He did not like this—no man would have liked it; and to Lionel the memory of an undignified act was acute torture. Why had he bidden the girls adieu and departed? Why had he, in fact, run away? What precisely would May Lawton think of him? How could he explain his conduct to her—and to himself? And had that worshipping, affectionate thing, May Deane, taken note of his confusion—of the confusion of him who was never confused, who was equal to every occasion and every emergency? These were some of the questions which harried him and declined to be settled. He had walked to Manifold, and had tea at the Roebuck, and walked back, and still the questions were harrying; and as he came over the hill by the field-path, and descried the lone house of the Deanes in the light of the Red Cow furnaces and of the moon, the worship of May Deane seemed suddenly very precious to him, and he could not bear to think that any stupidity of his should have impaired it.

Then he saw May Deane walking slowly across the field, close to an abandoned pit-shaft, whose low protecting circular wall of brick was crumbling to ruin on the side nearest to him.

She stopped, appeared to gaze at him intently, turned, and began to approach him. And he too, moved by a mysterious impulse which he did not pause to examine, swerved, and quickened his step in order to lessen the distance between them. He did not at first even feel surprise that she should be wandering solitary on the hill at that hour. Presently she stood still, while he continued to move forward. It was as if she drew him; and soon, in the pale moonlight and the wavering light of the furnaces, he could decipher all the details of her face, and he saw that she was smiling fondly, invitingly, admiringly, lustrously, with the old undiminished worship and affection. And he perceived a dark discoloration on her right cheek, as though she had suffered a blow, but this mark did not long occupy his mind. He thought suddenly of the strong probability that her father would leave a nice little bit of money to each of his three children; and he thought of her beauty, and of her timid fragility in the tight black dress, and of her immense and unquestioning love for him, which would survive all accidents and mishaps. He seemed to sink luxuriously into this grand passion of hers (which he deemed quite natural and proper) as into a soft feather-bed. To live secure in an atmosphere of exhaustless worship; to keep a fount of balm and admiration for ever in the house, a bubbling spring of passionate appreciation which would be continually available for the refreshment of his self-esteem! To be always sure of an obedience blind and willing, a subservience which no tyranny and no harshness and no whim would rouse into revolt; to sit on a throne with so much beauty kneeling at his feet!

And the possession of her beauty would be a source of legitimate pride to him. People would often refer to the beautiful Mrs. Woolley.

He felt that in sending May Deane to interrupt his highly emotional conversation with May Lawton Providence had watched over him and done him a good turn. May Lawton had advantages, and striking advantages, but he could not be sure of her. The suspicion that if she married him she would marry him for her own ends caused him a secret disquiet, and he feared that one day, perhaps one morning at breakfast, she might take it into her intelligent head to mock him, to exercise upon him her gift of irony, and to intimate to him that if he fancied she was his slave he was deceived. That she sincerely admired him he never for an instant doubted. But——

And, moreover, the unfortunate episode of the afternoon might have cooled her ardour to freezing-point.

He stood now in front of his worshipper, and the notion crossed his mind that in after-years he could say to his friends: 'I proposed to my wife at midnight under the moon. Not many men have done that.'

'Good-evening,' he ventured to the girl; and he added with bravado: 'We've met before to-day, haven't we?'

She made no reply, but her smile was more affectionate, more inviting, than ever.

'I'm glad of this opportunity—very glad,' he proceeded. 'I've been wanting to ... You must know, my dear girl, how I feel....'

She gave a gesture, charming in its sweet humility, as if to say: 'Who am I that I should dare——'

And then he proposed to her, asked her to share his life, and all that sort of thing; and when he had finished he thought, 'It's done now, anyway.'

Strange to relate, she offered no immediate reply, but she bent a little towards him with shining, happy eyes. He had an impulse to seize her in his arms and kiss her, but prudence suggested that he should defer the rite. She turned and began to walk slowly and meditatively towards the pit-shaft. He followed almost at her side, but a foot or so behind, waiting for her to speak. And as he waited, expectant, he looked at her profile and reflected how well the name May suited her, with its significances of shyness and dreamy hope, and hidden fire and the modesty of spring.

And while he was thus savouring her face, and they were still ten yards from the pit-shaft, she suddenly disappeared from his vision, as it were by a conjuring trick. He had a horrible sensation in his spinal column. He was not the man to mistrust the evidence of his senses, and he knew, therefore, that he had been proposing to a phantom.

V

The next morning—early, because of Jim's early breakfast—when May Deane's disappearance became known to the members of the household, Jim had the idea of utilizing Carlo in the search for her. The retriever went straight, without a fault, to the pit-shaft, and May was discovered alive and unscathed, save for a contusion of the face and a sprain in the wrist.

Her suicidal plunge had been arrested, at only a few feet from the top of the shaft, by a cross-stay of timber, upon which she lay prone. There was no reason why the affair should be made public, and it was not. It was suppressed into one of those secrets which embed themselves in the history of families, and after two or three generations blossom into romantic legends full of appropriate circumstantial detail.

Lionel Woolley spent a woeful night at his rooms. He did not know what to do, and on the following day May Lawton encountered him again, and proved by her demeanour that the episode of the previous afternoon had caused no estrangement. Lionel vacillated. The sway of the schoolmistress was almost restored, and it would have been restored fully had he not been preoccupied by a feverish curiosity—the curiosity to know whether or not May Deane was dead. He felt that she must indeed be dead, and he lived through the day expectant of the news of her sudden decease. Towards night his state of mind was such that he was obliged to call at the Deanes'. May heard him, and insisted on seeing him; more, she insisted on seeing him alone in the breakfast-room, where she reclined, interestingly white, on the sofa. Her father and brothers objected strongly to the interview, but they yielded, afraid that a refusal might induce hysteria and worse things.

And when Lionel Woolley came into the room, May, steeped in felicity, related to him the story of her impulsive crime.

'I was so happy,' she said, 'when I knew that Miss Lawton had deceived me.' And before he could inquire what she meant, she continued rapidly: 'I must have been unconscious, but I felt you were there, and something of me went out towards you. And oh! the answer to your question—I heard your question; the real *me* heard it, but that *something* could not speak.'

'My question?'

'You asked a question, didn't you?' she faltered, sitting up.

He hesitated, and then surrendered himself to her immense love and sank into it, and forgot May Lawton.

'Yes,' he said.

'The answer is yes. Oh, you must have known the answer would be yes! You did know, didn't you?'

He nodded grandly.

She sighed with delicious and overwhelming joy.

In the ecstasy of the achievement of her desire the girl gave little thought to the psychic aspect of the possibly unique wooing.

As for Lionel, he refused to dwell on it even in thought. And so that strange, magic, yearning effluence of a soul into a visible projection and shape was ignored, slurred over, and, after ten years of domesticity in the bank premises, is gradually being forgotten.

He is a man of business, and she, with her fading beauty, her ardent, continuous worship of the idol, her half-dozen small children, the eldest of whom is only eight, and the white window-curtains to change every week because of the smuts—do you suppose she has time or inclination to ponder upon the theory of the subliminal consciousness and kindred mysteries?

TIDDY-FOL-LOL

It was the dinner-hour, and a group of ragged and clay-soiled apprentice boys were making a great noise in the yard of Henry Mynors and Co.'s small, compact earthenware manufactory up at Toft End. Toft End caps the ridge to the east of Bursley; and Bursley, which has been the home of the potter for ten centuries, is the most ancient of the Five Towns in Staffordshire. The boys, dressed for the most part in shirt, trousers, and boots, all equally ragged and insecure, were playing at prison-bars.

Soon the game ended abruptly in a clamorous dispute upon a point of law, and it was not recommenced. The dispute dying a natural death, the tireless energies of the boys needed a fresh outlet. Inspired by a common instinct, they began at once to bait one of their number, a slight youngster of twelve years, much better clothed than the rest, who had adventurously strolled in from a neighbouring manufactory. This child answered their jibes in an amiable, silly, drawling tone which seemed to justify the epithet 'Loony,' frequently applied to him. Now and then he stammered; and then companions laughed loud, and he with them. It was known that several years ago he had fallen down a flight of stone steps, alighting on the back of his head, and that ever since he had been deaf of one ear and under some trifling mental derangement. His sublime calmness under their jests baffled them until the terrible figure of Mr. Machin, the engine-man, standing at the door of the slip-house, caught their attention and suggested a plan full of joyous possibilities. They gathered round the lad, and, talking in subdued murmurs, unanimously urged him with many persuasions to a certain course of action. He declined the scheme, and declined again. Suddenly a boy shouted:

'Thee dars' na'!'

'I dare,' was the drawled, smiling answer.

'I tell thee thee dars' na'!'

'I tell thee I dare.' And thereupon he slowly but resolutely set out for the slip-house door and Mr. Machin.

Eli Machin was beyond doubt the most considerable employé on Clarke's 'bank' (manufactory). Even Henry Clarke approached him with a subtly-indicated deference, and whenever Silas Emery, the immensely rich and miserly sleeping partner in the firm, came up to visit the works, these two old men chatted as old friends. In a modern earthenware manufactory the engine-room is the source of all activity, for, owing to the inventive genius of a famous and venerable son of the Five Towns, steam now presides at nearly every stage in the long process of turning earth into ware. It moves the pug-mill, the jollies, and the marvellous batting machines, dries the unfired clay, heats the printers' stoves, and warms the offices where the 'jacket-men' dwell. Coal is a tremendous item in the cost of production, and a competent, economical engine-man can be sure of good wages and a choice of berths; he is desired like a good domestic servant. Eli Machin was the prince of engine-men. His engine never went wrong, his coal bills were never extravagant, and (supreme virtue!) he was never absent on Mondays. From his post in the slip-house he watched over the whole works like a father, stern, gruff, forbidding, but to be trusted absolutely. He was sixty years old, and had been 'putting by' for nearly half a century. He lived in a tiny villa-cottage with his bed-ridden, cheerful wife, and lent small sums on mortgage of approved freeholds at 5 per cent.—no more and no less. Secure behind this rampart of saved money, he was the equal of the King on the throne. Not a magnate in all the Five Towns who would dare to be condescending to Eli Machin. He had been a sidesman at the old church. A trades-union had once asked him to become a working-man candidate for the Bursley Town Council, but he had refused because he did not care for the possibility of losing caste by being concerned in a strike. His personal respectability was entirely unsullied, and he worshipped this abstract quality as he worshipped God.

There was only one blot—but how foul!—on Eli Machin's career, and that had been dropped by his daughter Miriam, when, defying his authority, she married a scene-shifter at Hanbridge Theatre. The atrocious idea of being connected with the theatre had rendered him speechless for a time. He could but endure it in the most awful silence that ever hid passionate feeling. Then one day he had burst out, 'The wench is no better than a tiddy-fol-lol!' Only this solitary phrase—nothing else.

What a tiddy-fol-lol was no one quite knew; but the word, getting about, stuck to him, and for some weeks boys used to shout it after him in the streets, until he caught one of them, and in thirty seconds put an end to the practice. Thenceforth Miriam, with all hers, was dead to him. When her husband expired of consumption, Eli Machin saw the avenging arm of the Lord in action; and when her boy grew to be a source of painful anxiety to her, he said to himself that the wrath of Heaven was not yet cooled towards this impious daughter. The passage of fifteen years had apparently in no way softened his resentment.

The challenged lad in Mynors' yard slowly approached the slip-house door, and halted before Eli Machin, grinning.

'Well, young un,' the old man said absently, 'what dost want?'

'Tiddy-fol-lol, grandfeyther,' the child drawled in his silly, irritating voice, and added: 'They said I darena say it to ye.'

Without and instant's hesitation Eli Machin raised his still powerful arm, and, catching the boy under the ear, knocked him down. The other boys yelled with unaffected pleasure and ran away.

'Get up, and be off wi' ye. Ye dunna belong to this bank,' said Eli Machin in cold anger to the lad. But the lad did not stir; the lad's eyes were closed, and he lay white on the stones.

Eli Machin bent down, and peered through his spectacles at the prone form upon which the mid-day sun was beating.

'It's Miriam's boy!' he ejaculated under his breath, and looked round as if in inquiry—the yard was empty. Then with quick decision he picked up this limp and inconvenient parcel of humanity and hastened—ran—with it out of the yard into the road.

Down the road he ran, turned to the left into Clowes Street, and stopped before a row of small brown cottages. At the open door of one of these cottages a woman sat sewing. She was rather stout and full-bosomed, with a fair, fresh face, full of sense and peace; she looked under thirty, but was older.

'Here's thy Tommy, Miriam,' said Eli Machin shortly. 'He give me some of his sauce, and I doubt I've done him an injury.'

The woman dropped her sewing.

'Eh, dear!' she cried, 'is that lad o' mine in mischief again? I do hope he's no limb brokken.'

'It in'na that,' said the old man, 'but he's dazed-like. Better lay him on th' squab.'

She calmly took Tommy and placed him gently down on the check-covered sofa under the window. 'Come in, father, do.'

The man obeyed, astonished at the entire friendliness of this daughter, whom, though he had frequently seen her, he had never spoken to for more than ten years. Her manner, at once filial and quite natural, perfectly ignored the long breach, and disclosed no trace of animosity.

Father and daughter examined the unconscious child. Pale, pulseless, cold, he lay on the sofa like a corpse except for the short, faint breaths which he drew through his blue lips.

'I doubt I've killed him,' said Eli.

'Nay, nay, father!' And her face actually smiled. This supremacy of the soul against years of continued misfortune lifted her high above him, and he suddenly felt himself an inferior creature.

'I'll go for th' doctor,' he said.

'Nay! I shall need ye.' And she put her head out of the window. 'Mrs. Walley, will ye let your Lucy run quick for th' club doctor? my Tommy's hurt.'

The whole street awoke instantly from its nap, and in a few moments every door was occupied. Miriam closed her own door softly, as though she might wake the boy, and spoke in whispers to people through the window, finally telling them to go away. When the doctor came, half an hour afterwards, she had done all that she knew for Tommy, without the slightest apparent result.

'What is it?' asked the doctor curtly, as he lifted the child's thin and lifeless hand.

Eli Machin explained that he had boxed the boy's ear.

'Tommy was impudent to his grandfather,' Miriam added hastily.

'Which ear?' the doctor inquired. It was the left. He gazed into it, and then raised the boy's right leg and arm. 'There is no paralysis,' he said. Then he felt the heart, and then took out his stethoscope and applied it, listening intently.

'Canst hear owt?' the old man said.

'I cannot,' he answered.

'Don't say that, doctor—don't say that! said Miriam, with an accent of appeal.

'In these cases it is almost impossible to tell whether the patient is alive or dead. We must wait. Mrs. Baddeley, make a mustard plaster for his feet, and we will put another over the heart.' And so they waited one hour, while the clock ticked and the mustard plasters gradually cooled. Then Tommy's lips parted.

After another half-hour the doctor said:

'I must go now; I will come again at six. Do nothing but apply fresh plasters. Be sure to keep his neck free. He is breathing, but I may as well be plain with you—there is a great risk of your child dying in this condition.'

Neighbours were again at the window, and Miriam drew the blind, waving them away. At six o'clock the doctor reappeared. 'There is no change,' he remarked. 'I will call in before I go to bed.'

When he lifted the latch for the third time, at ten o'clock, Eli Machin and Miriam still sat by the sofa, and Tommy still lay thereon, moveless, a terrible enigma. But the glass lamp was lighted on the mantelpiece, and Miriam's sewing, by which she earned a livelihood, had been hidden out of sight.

'There is no change,' said the doctor. 'You can do nothing except hope.'

'And pray,' the calm mother added.

Eli neither stirred nor spoke. For nine hours he had absolutely forgotten his engine. He knew the boy would die.

The clock struck eleven, twelve, one, two, three, each time fretting the nerves of the old man like a rasp. It was the hour of summer dawn. A cold gray light fell unkindly across the small figure on the sofa.

'Open th' door a bit, father,' said Miriam. 'This parlour's gettin' close; th' lad canna breathe.'

'Nay, lass,' Eli sighed, as he stumbled obediently to the door. 'The lad'll breathe no more. I've killed him i' my anger.' He frowned heavily, as though someone was annoying him.

'Hist!' she exclaimed, when, after extinguishing the lamp, she returned to her boy's side. 'He's reddened—he's reddened! Look thee at his cheeks, father!' She seized the child's inert hands and rubbed them between her own. The blood was now plain in Tommy's face. His legs faintly twitched. His breathing was slower. Miriam moved the coverlet and put her head upon his heart. 'It's beating loud, father,' she cried. 'Bless God!'

Eli stared at the child with the fixity of a statue. Then Tommy opened his eyes for an instant. The old man groaned. Tommy looked vacantly round, closed his eyes again, and was unmistakably asleep. He slept for one minute, and then waked. Eli involuntarily put a hand on the sofa. Tommy gazed at him, and, with the most heavenly innocent smile of recognition, lightly touched his grandfather's hand. Then he turned over on his right side. In the anguish of sudden joy Eli gave a deep, piteous sob. That smile burnt into him like a coal of fire.

'Now for the beef-tea,' said Miriam, crying.

'Beef-tea?' the boy repeated after her, mildly questioning.

'Yes, my poppet,' she answered; and then aside, 'Father, he can hear i' his left ear. Did ye notice it?'

'It's a miracle—a miracle of God!' said Eli.

In a few hours Tommy was as well as ever—indeed, better; not only was his hearing fully restored, but he had ceased to stammer, and the thin, almost imperceptible cloud upon his intellect was dissipated. The doctor expressed but little surprise at these phenomena, and, in fact, stated that similar things had occurred often before, and were duly written down in the books of medicine. But Eli Machin's firm, instinctive faith that Providence had intervened will never be shaken.

Miriam and Tommy now live in the villa-cottage with the old people.

THE IDIOT

William Froyle, ostler at the Queen's Arms at Moorthorne, took the letter, and, with a curt nod which stifled the loquacity of the village postman, went at once from the yard into the coach-house. He had recognised the hand-writing on the envelope, and the recognition of it gave form and quick life to all the vague suspicions that had troubled him some months before, and again during the last few days. He felt suddenly the near approach of a frightful calamity which had long been stealing towards him.

A wire-sheathed lantern, set on a rough oaken table, cast a wavering light round the coach-house, and dimly showed the inner stable. Within the latter could just be distinguished the mottled-gray flanks of a fat cob which dragged its chain occasionally, making the large slow movements of a horse comfortably lodged in its stall. The pleasant odour of animals and hay filled the wide spaces of the shed, and through the half-open door came a fresh thin mist rising from the rain-soaked yard in the November evening.

Froyle sat down on the oaken table, his legs dangling, and looked again at the envelope before opening it. He was a man about thirty years of age, with a serious and thoughtful, rather heavy countenance. He had a long light moustache, and his skin was a fresh, rosy salmon colour; his straw-tinted hair was cut very short, except over the forehead, where it grew full and bushy. Dressed in his rough stable corduroys, his forearms bare and white, he had all the appearance of the sturdy Englishman, the sort of Englishman that crosses the world in order to find vent for his taciturn energy on virgin soils. From the whole village he commanded and received respect. He was known for a scholar, and it was his scholarship which had obtained for him the proud position of secretary to the provident society styled the Queen's Arms Slate Club. His respectability and his learning combined had enabled him to win with dignity the hand of Susie Trimmer, the grocer's daughter, to whom he had been engaged about a year. The village could not make up its mind concerning that match; without doubt it was a social victory for Froyle, but everyone wondered that so sedate and sagacious a man should have seen in Susie a suitable mate.

He tore open the envelope with his huge forefinger, and, bending down towards the lantern, began to read the letter. It ran:

'OLDCASTLE STREET,
'BURSLEY.
'DEAR WILL,

'I asked father to tell you, but he would not. He said I must write. Dear Will, I hope you will never see me again. As you will see by the above address, I am now at Aunt Penrose's at Bursley. She is awful angry, but I was obliged to leave the village because of my shame. I have been a wicked girl. It was in July. You know the man, because you asked me about him one Sunday night. He is no

good. He is a villain. Please forget all about me. I want to go to London. So many people know me here, and what with people coming in from the village, too. Please forgive me.

'S. TRIMMER.'

After reading the letter a second time, Froyle folded it up and put it in his pocket. Beyond a slight unaccustomed pallor of the red cheeks, he showed no sign of emotion. Before the arrival of the postman he had been cleaning his master's bicycle, which stood against the table. To this he returned. Kneeling down in some fresh straw, he used his dusters slowly and patiently—rubbing, then stopping to examine the result, and then rubbing again. When the machine was polished to his satisfaction, he wheeled it carefully into the stable, where it occupied a stall next to that of the cob. As he passed back again, the animal leisurely turned its head and gazed at Froyle with its large liquid eyes. He slapped the immense flank. Content, the animal returned to its feed, and the weighted chain ran down with a rattle.

The fortnightly meeting of the Slate Club was to take place at eight o'clock that evening. Froyle had employed part of the afternoon in making ready his books for the event, to him always so solemn and ceremonious; and the affairs of the club were now prominent in his mind. He was sorry that it would be impossible for him to attend the meeting; fortunately, all the usual preliminaries were complete.

He took a piece of notepaper from a little hanging cupboard, and, sprawling across the table, began to write under the lantern. The pencil seemed a tiny toy in his thick roughened fingers:

'*To Mr. Andrew McCall, Chairman Queen's Arms Slate Club.*

'DEAR SIR,

'I regret to inform you that I shall not be at the meeting to-night. You will find the' books in order....'

Here he stopped, biting the end of the pencil in thought. He put down the pencil and stepped hastily out of the stable, across the yard, and into the hotel. In the large room, the room where cyclists sometimes took tea and cold meat during the summer season, the long deal table and the double line of oaken chairs stood ready for the meeting. A fire burnt warmly in the big grate, and the hanging lamp had been lighted. On the wall was a large card containing the rules of the club, which had been written out in a fair hand by the schoolmaster. It was to this card that Froyle went. Passing his thumb down the card, he paused at Rule VII.:

'Each member shall, on the death of another member, pay 1s. for benefit of widow or nominee of deceased, same to be paid within one month after notice given.'

'Or nominee—nominee,' he murmured reflectively, staring at the card. He mechanically noticed, what he had noticed often before

with disdain, that the chairman had signed the rules without the use of capitals.

He went back to the dusk of the coach-house to finish his letter, still murmuring the word 'nominee,' of whose meaning he was not quite sure:

'I request that the money due to me from the Slate Club on my death shall be paid to my nominee, Miss Susan Trimmer, now staying with her aunt, Mrs. Penrose, at Bursley.

'Yours respectfully,
'WILLIAM FROYLE.'
After further consideration he added:

'P.S.—My annual salary of sixpence per member would be due at the end of December. If so be the members would pay that, or part of it, should they consider the same due, to Susan Trimmer as well, I should be thankful.—Yours resp, W.F.'

He put the letter in an envelope, and, taking it to the large room, laid it carefully at the end of the table opposite the chairman's seat. Once more he returned to the coach-house. From the hanging cupboard he now produced a piece of rope. Standing on the table he could just reach, by leaning forward, a hook in the ceiling, that was sometimes used for the slinging of bicycles. With difficulty he made the rope fast to the hook. Putting a noose on the other end, he tightened it round his neck. He looked up at the ceiling and down at the floor in order to judge whether the rope was short enough.

'Good-bye, Susan, and everyone,' he whispered, and then stepped off the table.

The tense rope swung him by his neck halfway across the coach-house. He swung twice to and fro, but as he passed under the hook for the fifth time his toes touched the floor. The rope had stretched. In another second he was standing firm on the floor, purple and panting, but ignominiously alive.

'Good-even to you, Mr. Froyle. Be you committing suicide?' The tones were drawling, uncertain, mildly astonished.

He turned round hastily, his hands busy with the rope, and saw in the doorway the figure of Daft Jimmy, the Moorthorne idiot.

He hesitated before speaking, but he was not confused. No one could have been confused before Daft Jimmy. Neither man nor woman in the village considered his presence more than that of a cat.

'Yes, I am,' he said.

The middle-aged idiot regarded him with a vague, interested smile, and came into the coach-house.

'You'n gotten the rope too long, Mr. Froyle. Let me help you.'

Froyle calmly assented. He stood on the table, and the two rearranged the noose and made it secure. As they did so the idiot gossiped:

'I was going to Bursley to-night to buy me a pair o' boots, and when I was at top o' th' hill I remembered as I'd forgotten the measure o' my feet. So I ran back again for it. Then I saw the light in here, and I stepped up to bid ye good-evening.'

Someone had told him the ancient story of the fool and his boots, and, with the pride of an idiot in his idiocy, he had determined that it should be related of himself.

Froyle was silent.

The idiot laughed with a dry cackle.

'Now you go,' said Froyle, when the rope was fixed.

'Let me see ye do it,' the idiot pleaded with pathetic eyes.

'No; out you get!'

Protesting, the idiot went forth, and his irregular clumsy footsteps sounded on the pebble-paved yard. When the noise of them ceased in the soft roadway, Froyle jumped off the table again. Gradually his body, like a stopping pendulum, came to rest under the hook, and hung twitching, with strange disconnected movements. The horse in the stable, hearing unaccustomed noises, rattled his chain and stamped about in the straw of his box.

Furtive steps came down the yard again, and Daft Jimmy peeped into the coach-house.

'He done it! he done it!' the idiot cried gleefully. 'Damned if he hasna'.' He slapped his leg and almost danced. The body still twitched occasionally. 'He done it!'

'Done what, Daft Jimmy? You're making a fine noise there! Done what?'

The idiot ran out of the stable. At the side-entrance to the hotel stood the barmaid, the outline of her fine figure distinct against the light from within.

The idiot continued to laugh.

'Done what?' the girl repeated, calling out across the dark yard in clear, pleasant tones of amused inquiry. 'Done what?'

'What's that to you, Miss Tucker?'

'Now, none of your sauce, Daft Jimmy! Is Willie Froyle in there?'

The idiot roared with laughter.

'Yes, he is, miss.'

'Well, tell him his master wants him. I don't want to cross this mucky, messy yard.'

'Yes, miss.'

The girl closed the door.

The idiot went into the coach-house, and, slapping William's body in a friendly way so that it trembled on the rope, he spluttered out between his laughs:

'Master wants ye, Mr. Froyle.'

Then he walked out into the village street, and stood looking up the muddy road, still laughing quietly. It was quite dark, but the moon aloft in the clear sky showed the highway with its shining ruts leading in a straight line over the hill to Bursley.

'Them shoes!' the idiot ejaculated suddenly. 'Well, I be an idiot, and that's true! They can take the measure from my feet, and I never thought on it till this minute!'

Laughing again, he set off at a run up the hill.

PART II
ABROAD

THE HUNGARIAN RHAPSODY

I

After a honeymoon of five weeks in the shining cities of the Mediterranean and in Paris, they re-entered the British Empire by the august portals of the Chatham and Dover Railway. They stood impatiently waiting, part of a well-dressed, querulous crowd, while a few officials performed their daily task of improvising a Custom-house for registered luggage on a narrow platform of Victoria Station. John, Mr. Norris's man, who had met them, attended behind. Suddenly, with a characteristic movement, the husband lifted his head, and then looked down at his wife.

'I say, May!'

'Well?'

She knew that he was about to propose some swift alteration of their plans, but she smiled upwards out of her furs at his grave face, and the tone of her voice granted all requests in advance.

'I think I'd better go to the office,' he said.

'Now?'

She smiled again, inviting him to do exactly what he chose. She was already familiar with his restiveness under enforced delays and inaction, and his unfortunate capacity for being actively bored by trifles which did not interest him aroused in her a sort of maternal sympathy.

'Yes,' he answered. 'I can be there and back in an hour or less. You titivate yourself, and we'll dine at the Savoy, or anywhere you please. We'll keep the ball rolling to-night. Yes,' he repeated, as if to convince himself that he was not a deserter, 'I really must call in at the office. You and John can see to the luggage, can't you?'

'Of course,' she replied, with calm good-nature, and also with perfect self-confidence. 'But give me the keys of the trunks, and don't be late, Ted.'

'Oh, I shan't be late,' he said.

Their fingers touched as she took the keys. He went away enraptured anew by her delightful acquiescences, her unique smile, her common-sense, her mature charm, and the astonishing elegance of her person. The honeymoon was over— and with what finished discretion, combining the innocent girl with the woman of the world, she had lived through the honeymoon!—another life, more delicious, was commencing.

'What a wife!' he thought triumphantly. 'She does understand a man! And fancy leaving any ordinary bride to look after luggage!'

Nevertheless, once in his offices at Winchester House, he managed to forget her, and to forget time, for nearly an hour and a half. When at last he came to himself from the enchantment of affairs, he jumped into a hansom, and told the driver to drive fast to Knightsbridge. He was ardent to see her again. In the dark seclusion of the cab he speculated upon her toilette, the colour of her shoes. He thought of the last five weeks, of the next five years. Dwelling on their mutual love and esteem, their health, their self-knowledge and experience and cheerfulness, her sense and grace, his talent for getting money first and keeping it afterwards, he foresaw nothing but happiness for them. Children? H'm! Possibly....

At Piccadilly Circus it began to rain—cold, heavy March rain.

'Window down, sir?' asked the voice of the cabman.

'Yes,' he ordered sardonically. 'Better be suffocated than drowned.'

'You're right, sir,' said the voice.

Soon, through the streaming glass, which made every gas-jet into a shooting pillar of flame, Norris discerned vaguely the vast bulk of Hyde Park Mansions. 'Good!' he muttered, and at that very moment he was shot through the window into the thin, light-reflecting mire of the street. Enormous and strange beasts menaced him with pitiless hoofs. Millions of people crowded about him. In response to a question that seemed to float slowly towards him, he tried to give his address. He realized, by a considerable feat of intellect, that the horse must have fallen down; and then, with a dim notion that nothing mattered, he went to sleep.

II

In the boudoir of the magnificent flat on the first floor, shielded from the noise and the inclemency of the world by four silk-hung walls and a double window, and surrounded by all the multitudinous and costly luxury that a stockbroker with brains and taste can obtain for the wife of his love, May was leisurely finishing her toilette. And every detail in the long, elaborate process was accomplished with a passionate intention to bewitch the man at Winchester House.

These two had first met seven years before, when May, the daughter of a successful wholesale draper at Hanbridge, in the Five Towns district of Staffordshire, was aged twenty-two. Mr. Scarratt went to Manchester each Tuesday to buy, and about once a month he took May with him. One day, when they were lunching at the Exchange Restaurant, a young man came up whom her father introduced as Mr. Edward Norris, his stockbroker. Mr. Norris, whose years were thirty, glanced keenly at May, and accepted Mr. Scarratt's invitation to join them. Ever afterwards May vividly remembered the wonderful sensation, joyous yet disconcerting, which she then experienced—the sensation of having captivated her father's handsome and correct stockbroker. The three talked horses with a certain freedom, and since May was accustomed to drive the Scarratt dogcart, so famous in the Five Towns, she could bring her due share to the conversation. The meal over, Mr. Norris discussed business matters with his client, and then sedately departed, but not without the obviously sincere expression of a desire to meet Miss Scarratt again. The wholesale draper praised Edward's financial qualities behind his back, and wondered that a man of such aptitude should remain in Manchester while London existed. As for May, she decided that she would have a new frock before she came to Manchester in the following month.

She had a new frock, but not of the colour intended. By the following month her father was enclosed in a coffin, and it happened to his estate, as to the estates of many successful men who employ stockbrokers, that the liabilities far more than covered the assets. May and her mother were left without a penny. The mother did the right thing, and died—it was best. May went direct to Brunt's, the largest draper in the Five Towns, and asked for a place under 'Madame' in the dress-making department. Brunt's daughter, who was about to be married, gave her the place instantly. Three years later, when 'Madame' returned to Paris, May stepped into the French-woman's shoes.

On Sundays and on Thursday afternoons, and sometimes (but not too often) at the theatre, May was the finest walking advertisement that Brunt's ever had. Old Brunt would have proposed to her, it was rumoured, had he not been scared by her elegance. Sundry sons of prosperous manufacturers, unabashed by this elegance, did in fact secretly propose, but with what result was known only to themselves.

Later, as May waxed in importance at Brunt's, she was sent to Manchester to buy. She lunched at the Exchange Restaurant. The world and Manchester are very small. The first man she set eyes on was Edward Norris. Another week, Norris said to her with a thrill, and he would have been gone for ever to London. Chance is not to be flouted. The sequel was inevitable. They loved. And all the select private bars in Hanbridge tinkled to the news that May Scarratt had been and hooked a stockbroker!

When the toilette was done, and the maid gone, she wound a thin black scarf round her olive neck and shoulders, and sat down negligently on a Chippendale settee in the attitude of a portrait by Boldini; her little feet were tucked up sideways on the settee; the perforated lace ends of the scarf fell over her low corsage to the level of the seat. And she waited, still the bride. He was late, but she knew he would be late. Sure in the conviction that he was a strong man, a man of imagination and of deeds, she could easily excuse this failing in him, as she did that other habit of impulsive action in trifles. Nay, more, she found keen pleasure in excusing it. 'Dear thing!' she reflected, 'he forgets so.' Therefore she waited, content in enjoying the image in the glass of her dark face, her small plump person, and her Paris gown—that dream! She thought with assuaged grief of her father's tragedy; she would have liked him to see her now, the jewel in the case—her father and she had understood each other.

All around, and above and below, she felt, without hearing it, the activity of the opulent, complex life of the mansions. Her mind dwelt with satisfaction on long carpeted corridors noiselessly paraded by flunkeys, mahogany lifts continually ascending and descending like the angels of the ladder, the great entrance hall with its fire always burning and its doors always swinging, the *salle à manger* sown with rose-shaded candles, and all the splendid privacies rising stage upon stage to the attics, where the flunkeys philosophized together. She confessed the beauty and distinction achieved by this extravagant organization for gratifying earthly desires. Often, in the pinching days of her servitude, she had murmured against the injustice of things, and had called wealth a crime while poverty starved. But now she perceived that society was what it was inevitably, and could not be altered. She accepted it in profound peace of mind, gaily fraternal towards the fortunate, compassionate towards those in adversity.

In the next flat someone began to play very brilliantly a Hungarian Rhapsody of Liszt's. And even the faint sound of that riotous torrent of melody, so arrogantly gorgeous, intoxicated her soul. She shivered under the sudden vision of the splendid joy of being alive. And how she envied the player! French she had learned from 'Madame,' but she had no skill on the piano; it was her one regret.

She touched the bell.

'Has your master come in yet?' she inquired of the maid.

'No, madam, not yet.'

She knew he had not come in, but she could not resist the impulse to ask.

Ten minutes later, when the piano had ceased, she jumped up, and, creeping to the front-door of the flat, gazed foolishly across the corridor at the grille of the lift. She heard the lift in travail. It appeared and passed out of sight above. No, he had not come! Glancing aside, she saw the tall slender figure of a girl in a green tea-gown—a mere girl: it was the player of the Hungarian Rhapsody. And this

82

girl, too, she thought, was expectant and disappointed! They shut their doors simultaneously, she and May, who also had her girlish moments. Then the rhapsody recommenced.

'Oh, madam!' screamed the maid, almost tumbling into the boudoir.

'What is it?' May demanded with false calm.

The maid lifted the corner of her black apron to her eyes, as though she had been a stage soubrette in trouble.

'The master, madam! He's fell out of his cab—just in front of the mansions— and they're bringing him in—such blood I never did see!'

The maid finished with hysterics.

III

'And them just off their honeymoon!'

The inconsolable tones of the lady's-maid came from the kitchen to the open door of the bedroom, where May was giving instructions to the elderly cook.

'Send that girl out of the flat this moment!' May said.

'Yes, ma'am.'

'Make the beef-tea in case it's wanted, and let me have some more warm water. There's John and the doctor!'

She started at a knock.

'No, it's only the postman, ma'am.'

Some letters danced on the hall floor and on her nerves.

'Oh dear!' May whispered. 'I thought it was the doctor at last.'

'John's bound to be back with one in a minute, ma'am. Do bear up,' urged the cook, hurrying to the kitchen.

She could have destroyed the woman for those last words.

With the proud certainty of being equal to the dreadful crisis, she turned abruptly into the bedroom, where her husband lay insensible on one of the new beds. Assisted by the policemen and the cook, she had done everything that could be done: cut away the coats and the waistcoat, removed the boots, straightened the limbs, washed the face and neck—especially the neck—which had to be sponged continually, and scattered messengers, including John, over the vicinity in search of medical aid. And now the policemen had gone, the general emotion on the staircase had subsided, the front-door of the flat was shut. The great ocean of the life of the mansions had closed smoothly upon her little episode. She was alone with the shattered organism.

She bent fondly over the bed, and her Paris frock, and the black scarf which she had not removed, touched its ruinous burden. Her right hand directed the sponge with ineffable tenderness, and then the long thin fingers tightened to a frenzied clutch to squeeze it over the basin. The whole of her being was absorbed in a deep passion of pity and an intolerable hunger for the doctor.

Through the wall came once more the faint sound of the Hungarian Rhapsody, astonishingly rapid and brilliant. She set her teeth to endure its unconscious message of the vast indifference of life to death.

The organism stirred, and May watched the deathly face for a sign. The eyes opened and stared at her in agonized bewilderment. The lips tried to speak, and failed.

'It's all right, darling,' she said softly. 'You're in your own bed. The doctor will be here directly. Drink this.'

She gave him some brandy-and-water, and they looked at each other. He was no longer Edward Norris, the finely regulated intelligence, the masterful volition, the conqueror of the world and of a woman; but merely the embodiment of a frightened, despairing, flickering, hysterical will-to-live, which glanced in terror at the corners of the room as though it saw fate there. And beneath her intense solicitude was the instinctive feeling, which hurt her, but which she could not dismiss, of her measureless, dominating superiority. With what glad relief would she have changed places with him!

'I'm dying, May,' he murmured at length, with a sigh. 'Why doesn't the doctor come?'

'He is coming,' she replied soothingly. 'You'll be better soon.'

But his effort in speaking obliged her to use the sponge again, and he saw it, and drew another sigh, more mortal than the first.

'Oh! I'm dying,' he repeated.

'Not you, Ted!' And her smile cost her an awful pang.

'I am. I know it.' This time he spoke with sad resignation. 'You must face it. And—listen.'

'What, dear?'

A physical sensation of sickness came over her. She could not disguise from herself the fact that he was dying. The warped and pallid face, the panic-struck eyes, the sweat, the wound in the neck, the damp hands nervously pulling the hem of the sheet—these indications were not to be gainsaid. The truth was too horrible to grasp; she wanted to put it away from her. 'This calamity cannot happen to me!' she thought urgently, and all the while she knew that it was happening to her.

He collected the feeble remnant of his powers by an immense effort, and began to speak, slowly and fragmentarily, and with such weakness that she could only catch his words by putting her ear to his mouth. The restless hands dropped the sheet and took the end of the black scarf.

'You'll be comfortable—for money,' he said. 'Will made.... It's not that. It's ... I must tell you. It's——'

'Yes?' she encouraged him. 'Tell me. I can hear.'

'It's about your father. I didn't treat him quite right ... once.... Week after I first met you, May.... No, not quite right. He was holding Hull and Barnsley shares ... you know, railway ... great gambling stock, then, Hull and Barn— Barnsley. Holding them on cover; for the rise.... They dropped too much— dropped to 23.... He couldn't hold any longer ... wired to me to sell and cut the loss. Understand?'

'Yes,' she said, trembling. 'I quite understand.'

'Well ... I wired back, "Sold at 23." ... But some mistake. Shares not sold. Clerk's mistake.... Clerk didn't sell.... Next day rise began.... I didn't wire him shares not sold. Somehow, I couldn't.... Put it off.... Rise went on.... I took over shares myself ... you see—myself.... Made nearly five thousand clear.... I wanted money then.... I think I would have told him, perhaps, later ... made it right ... but he died ... sudden ... I wasn't going to let his creditors have that five thou.... No, he'd meant to sell ... and, look here, May, if those shares had dropped lower ... 'stead of rising ... I should have had to stand the racket ... with your father, for my clerk's mistake.... See?... He'd meant to sell.... Hard lines on him, but he'd meant to sell.... He'd meant——'

'Don't say any more, dear.'

'Must explain this, May. Why didn't I give the money to you ... when he was dead?... Because I knew you'd only ... give it ... to creditors.... I knew you.... That's straight.... I've told you now.'

He lost consciousness again, but for an instant May did not notice it. She was crying, and her tears fell on his face.

Then came a doctor, a little dark man, who explained with calm politeness that he had been out when the messenger first arrived. He took off his coat, hung it up, opened his bag, and proceeded to a minute examination of the patient. His movements were so methodical, and he gave orders to May in a tone so quiet, casual, and ordinary, that she almost lost her sense of the reality of the scene.

'Yes, yes,' he said, from time to time, as if to himself; nothing else; not a single enlightening word to May.

'I'm dying,' moaned Edward, opening his eyes.

The doctor glanced round at May and winked. That wink, deliberate and humorous, was like an electric shock to her. She could actually feel her heart leap in her breast. If she had not been afraid of the doctor, she would have fainted.

'You all think you're dying,' the doctor remarked in a low, amused tone to the ceiling, as he wiped a pair of scissors, 'when you've been knocked silly, especially if there's a lot of blood about.'

The door opened.

'Here's John, ma'am,' said the cook, 'with two more doctors. What am I to do?'

May involuntarily turned towards the door.

'Don't you go, Mrs. Norris,' the little dark man commanded. 'I want you.' Then he carelessly scrutinized the elderly servant. 'Tell 'em they're too late,' he said. 'It's generally like that when there's an accident,' he continued after the housekeeper had gone. 'First you can't get a doctor anywhere, and then in half an hour or so we come in crowds. I've known seven doctors turn up one after another. But in that affair the man happened to have been killed outright.'

He smiled grimly. In a little while he was snapping his bag.

'I'll come in the morning, of course,' he said, as he wrote on a piece of paper. 'Have this made up, and give it him in the night if he is wakeful. Keep him warm. You might put a couple of hot-water bags, one on either side of him. You've got beef-tea made, you say? That's right. Let him have as much as he wants. Mr. Norris, you'll sleep like a top.'

'But, doctor,' May inquired the next morning in the hall, after Edward had smiled at a joke, and been informed that he must run down to Bournemouth in a week, 'have we nothing to fear?'

'I think not,' was the measured answer. 'These affairs nearly always seem much worse than they are. Of course, the immediate upset is tremendous—the disorganization, and all that sort of thing. But Nature's pretty wonderful. You'll find your husband will soon get over it. I should say he had a good constitution.'

'And there will be no permanent effects?'

'Yes,' said the doctor, with genial cynicism. 'There'll be one permanent effect. Nobody will ever persuade him to ride in a hansom again. If he can't find a four-wheeler, he'll walk in future.'

She returned to the bedroom. The man on the bed was Edward Norris once more, in control of himself, risen out of his humiliation. A feeling of thankfulness overwhelmed her for a moment, and she sat down.

'Well, May?' he murmured.

'Well, dear.'

They both realized that what they had been through was a common, daily street accident. The smile of each was self-conscious, apprehensive, insincere.

'Quite a concert going on next door,' he said with an affectation of lightness.

It was the Hungarian Rhapsody, impetuous and brilliant as ever. How she hated it now—this symbol of the hurried, unheeding, relentless, hollow gaiety of the world! Yet she longed for the magic fingers of the player, that she, too, might smother grief in such glittering veils!

IV

The marriage which had begun so dramatically fell into placid routine. Edward fulfilled the prophecy of the doctor. In a week they were able to go to Bournemouth for a few days, and in less than a fortnight he was at the office— the strong man again, confident and ambitious.

After days devoted to finance, he came home in the evenings high-spirited and determined to enjoy himself. His voice was firm and his eye steady when he spoke to his wife; there was no trace of self-consciousness in his demeanour. She admired the masculinity of the brain that could forget by an effort of will. She felt that he trusted her to forget also; that he relied on her common-sense, her characteristic sagacity, to extinguish for ever the memory of an awkward incident. He loved her. He was intensely proud of her. He treated her with every sort of generosity. And in return he expected her to behave like a man.

She loved him. She esteemed him as a wife should. She made a profession of wifehood. He gave his days to finance and his nights to diversion; but her vocation was always with her—she was never off duty. She aimed to please him to the uttermost in everything, to be in all respects the ideal helpmate of a husband who was at once strenuous, fastidious, and wealthy. Elegance and suavity were a religion with her. She was the delight of the eye and of the ear, the soother of groans, the refuge of distress, the uplifter of the heart.

She made new acquaintances for him, and cemented old friendships. Her manner towards his old friends enchanted him; but when they were gone she had a way of making him feel that she was only his. She thought that she was succeeding in her aim. She thought that all these sweet, endless labours—of traffic with dressmakers, milliners, coiffeurs, maids, cooks, and furnishers; of paying and receiving calls; of delicious surprise journeys to the City to bring home the breadwinner; of giving and accepting dinners; of sitting alert and appreciative in theatres and music-halls; of supping in golden restaurants; of being serious, cautionary, submissive, and seductive; of smiles, laughter, and kisses; and of continuous sympathetic responsiveness—she thought that all these labours had attained their object: Edward's complete serenity and satisfaction. She imagined that love and duty had combined successfully to deceive him on one solitary point. She was sure that he was deceived. But she was wrong.

One evening they were at the theatre alone together. It was a musical comedy, and they had a large stage-box. May sat a little behind. After having been darkened for a scenic conjuring trick, the stage was very suddenly thrown into brilliant light. Edward turned with equal suddenness to share his appreciation of the effect with his wife, and the light and his eye caught her unawares. She smiled instantly, but too late; he had seen the expression of her features. For a second she felt as if the whole fabric which she had been building for the last six months had crumbled; but this disturbing idea passed as she recovered herself.

'Let's go home, eh?' he said, at the end of the first act.

'Yes,' she agreed. 'It would be nice to be in early, wouldn't it?'

In the brougham they exchanged the amiable banalities of people who are thoroughly intimate. When they reached the flat, she poured out his whisky-and-potass, and sat on the arm of his particular arm-chair while he sipped it; then she whispered that she was going to bed.

'Wait a bit,' he said; 'I want to talk to you seriously.'

'Dear thing!' she murmured, stroking his coat.

She had not the slightest notion of his purpose.

'You've tried your best, May,' he said bluntly, 'but you've failed. I've suspected it for a long time.'

She flushed, and retired to a sofa, away from the orange electric lamp.

'What do you mean, Edward?' she asked.

'You know very well what I mean, my dear,' he replied. 'What I told you—that night! You've tried to forget it. You've tried to look at me as though you had forgotten it. But you can't do it. It's on your mind. I've noticed it again and again. I noticed it at the theatre to-night. So I said to myself, "I'll have it out with her." And I'm having it out.'

'My dear Ted, I assure you——'

'No, you don't,' he stopped her. 'I wish you did. Now you must just listen. I know exactly what sort of an idiot I was that night as well as you do. But I couldn't help it. I was a fool to tell you. Still, I thought I was dying. I simply had a babbling fit. People are like that. You thought I was dying, too, didn't you?'

'Yes,' she said quietly, 'for a minute or two.'

'Ah! It was that minute or two that did it. Well, I let it out, the rotten little secret. I admit it wasn't on the square, that bit of business. But, on the other hand, it wasn't anything really bad—like cruelty to animals or ruining a girl. Of course, the chap was your father, but, but——. Look here, May, you ought to be able to see that I was exactly the same man after I told you as I was before. You ought to be able to see that. My character wasn't wrecked because I happened to split on myself, like an ass, about that affair. Mind you, I don't blame you. You can't help your feelings. But do you suppose there's a single man on this blessed earth without a secret? I'm not going to grovel before gods or men. I'm not going to pretend I'm so frightfully sorry. I'm sorry in a way. But can't you see——'

'Don't say any more, Ted,' she begged him, fingering her sash. 'I know all that. I know it all, and everything else you can say. Oh, my darling boy! do you think I would look down on you ever so little because of—what you told me? Who am I? I wouldn't care twopence even if——'

'But it's between us all the same,' he broke in. 'You can't get over it.'

'Get over it!' she repeated lamely.

'Can you? Have you?' He pinned her to a direct answer.

She did not flinch.

'No,' she said.

'I thought you would have done,' he remarked, half to himself. 'I thought you would. I thought you were enough a woman of the world for that, May. It isn't as if the confounded thing had made any real difference to your father. The old man died, and——'

'Ted!' she exclaimed, 'I shall have to tell you, after all. It killed him.'

'What killed him? He died of gastritis.'

'He was ill with gastritis, but he died of suicide. It's easy for a gastritis patient to commit suicide. And father did.'

'Why?'

'Oh, ruin, despair! He'd been in difficulties for a long time. He said that selling those shares just one day too soon was the end of it. When he saw them going up day after day, it got on his mind. He said he knew he would never, never have any luck. And then ...'

'You kept it quiet.' He was walking about the room.

'Yes, that was pretty easy.'

'And did your mother know?'

He turned and looked at her.

'Yes, mother knew. It finished her. Oh, Ted!' she burst out, 'if you'd only telegraphed to him the next morning that the shares weren't sold, things might have been quite different.'

'You mean I killed your father—and your mother.'

'No, I don't,' she cried passionately. 'I tell you I don't. You didn't know. But I think of it all, sometimes. And that's why—that's why——'

She sat down again.

'By God, May,' he swore, 'I'm frightfully sorry!'

'I never meant to tell you,' she said, composing herself. 'But, there! things slip out. Good-night.'

She was gone, but in passing him she had timidly caressed his shoulder.

'It's all up,' he said to himself. 'This will always be between us. No one could expect her to forget it.'

V

Gradually her characteristic habits deserted her; she seemed to lose energy and a part of her interest in those things which had occupied her most. She changed her dress less frequently, ignoring dressmakers, and she showed no longer the ravishing elegance of the bride. She often lay in bed till noon, she who had always entered the dining-room at nine o'clock precisely to dispense his coffee and listen to his remarks on the contents of the newspaper. She said 'As you please' to the cook, and the meals began to lose their piquancy. She paid no calls, but some of her women friends continued, nevertheless, to visit her. Lastly, she took to sewing. The little dark doctor, who had become an acquaintance, smiled at her and told her to do no more than she felt disposed to do. She reclined on sofas in shaded rooms, and appeared to meditate. She was not depressed, but thoughtful. It was as though she had much to settle in her own mind. At intervals the faint sound of the Hungarian Rhapsody mingled with her reveries.

As for Edward, his behaviour was immaculate. During the day he made money furiously. In the evening he sat with his wife. They did not talk much, and he never questioned her. She developed a certain curious whimsicality now and then; but for him she could do no wrong.

The past was not mentioned. They both looked apprehensively towards the future, towards a crisis which they knew was inexorably approaching. They were afraid, while pretending to have no fear.

And one afternoon, precipitately, surprisingly, the crisis came.

'You are the father of a son—a very noisy son,' said the doctor, coming into the drawing-room where Edward had sat in torture for three hours.

'And May?'

'Oh, never fear: she's doing excellently.'

'Can I go and see her?' he asked, like a humble petitioner.

'Well—yes,' said the doctor, 'for one minute; not more.'

So he went into the bedroom as into a church, feeling a fool. The nurse, miraculously white and starched, stood like a sentinel at the foot of the bed of mystery.

'All serene, May?' he questioned. If he had attempted to say another word he would have cried.

The pale mother nodded with a fatigued smile, and by a scarcely perceptible gesture drew his attention to a bundle. From the next flat came a faint, familiar sound, insolently joyous.

'Yes,' he thought, 'but if they had both been lying dead here that tune would have been the same.'

Two months later he left the office early, telling his secretary that he had a headache. It was a mere fibbing excuse. He suffered from sudden fits of anxiety about his wife and child. When he reached the flat, he found no one at home but the cook.

'Where's your mistress?' he demanded.

'She's out in the park with baby and nurse, sir.'

'But it's going to rain,' he cried angrily. 'It is raining. They'll get wet through.'

He rushed into the corridor, and met the procession—May, the perambulator, and the nursemaid.

'Only fancy, Ted!' May exclaimed, 'the perambulator will go into the lift, after all. Aren't you glad?'

'Yes,' he said. 'But you're wet, surely?'

'Not a drop. We just got in in time.'

'Sure?'

'Quite.'

The tableau of May, elegant as ever, but her eyes brighter and her body more leniently curved, of the hooded perambulator, and of the fluffy-white nursemaid behind—it was too much for him. Touching clumsily the apron of the perambulator, the stockbroker turned into his doorway. Just then the girl from the next flat came out into the corridor, dressed for social rites of the afternoon. The perambulator was her excuse for stopping.

'What a pretty boy!' she exclaimed in ecstasy, trying to squeeze her picture hat under the hood of the perambulator.

'Do you really think so?' said the mother, enchanted.

'Of course! The darling! How I envy you!'

May wanted to reciprocate this politeness.

'I can't tell you,' she said, 'how I envy you your piano-playing. There's one piece——'

'Envy me! Why! It's only a pianola we've got!'

'Isn't he the picture of his granddad?' said May to Edward when they bent over the cot that night before retiring.

And as she said it there was such candour in her voice, such content in her smiling and courageous eyes, that Edward could not fail to comprehend her message to him. Down in some very secret part of his soul he felt for the first time the real force of the great explanatory truth that one generation succeeds another.

THE SISTERS QITA

The manuscript ran thus:

When I had finished my daily personal examination of the ropes and trapezes, I hesitated a moment, and then climbed up again, to the roof, where the red and the blue long ropes were fastened. I took my sharp scissors from my chatelaine, and gently fretted the blue rope with one blade of the scissors until only a single strand was left intact. I gazed down at the vast floor a hundred feet below. The afternoon varieties were over, and a phrenologist was talking to a small crowd of gapers in a corner. The rest of the floor was pretty empty save for the chairs and the fancy stalls, and the fatigued stall-girls in their black dresses. I too, had once almost been a stall-girl at the Aquarium! I descended. Few observed me in my severe street dress. Our secretary, Charles, attended me on the stage.

'Everything right, Miss Paquita?' he said, handing me my hat and gloves, which I had given him, to hold.

I nodded. I could see that he thought I was in one of my stern, far-away moods.

'Miss Mariquita is waiting for you in the carriage,' he said.

We drove away in silence—I with my inborn melancholy too sad, Sally (Mariquita) too happy to speak. This daily afternoon drive was really part of our 'turn'! A team of four mules driven by a negro will make a sensation even in Regent Street. All London looked at us, and contrasted our impassive beauty— mine mature (too mature!) and dark, Sally's so blonde and youthful, our simple costumes, and the fact that we stayed at an exclusive Mayfair hotel, with the stupendous flourish of our turnout. The renowned Sisters Qita—Paquita and Mariquita Qita—and the renowned mules of the Sisters Qita! Two hundred pounds a week at the Aquarium! Twenty-five thousand francs for one month at the Casino de Paris! Twelve thousand five hundred dollars for a tour of fifty performances in the States! Fifteen hundred pesos a night and a special train *de luxe* in Argentina and Brazil! I could see the loungers and the drivers talking and pointing as usual. The gilded loungers in Verrey's café got up and watched us through the windows as we passed. This was fame. For nearly twenty years I had been intimate with fame, and with the envy of women and the foolish homage of men.

We saw dozens of omnibuses bearing the legend 'Qita.' Then we met one which said: 'Empire Theatre. Valdès, the matchless juggler,' and Sally smiled with pleasure.

'He's coming to see our turn to-night, after his,' she remarked, blushing.

'Valdès? Why?' I asked, without turning my head.

'He wants us to sup with him, to celebrate our engagement.'

'When do you mean to get married?' I asked her shortly. I felt quite calm.

'I guess you're a Tartar to-day,' said the pretty thing, with a touch of her American sauciness. 'We haven't studied it out yet. It was only yesterday afternoon he kissed me for the first time.' Then she bent towards me with her characteristic plaintive, wistful appeal. 'Say! You aren't vexed, Selina, are you, because of this? Of course, he wants me to tour with him after we're married, and do a double act. He's got lots of dandy ideas for a double act. But I won't, I won't, Selina, unless you say the word. Now, don't you go and be cross, Selina.'

I let myself expand generously.

'My darling girl!' I said, glancing at her kindly. 'You ought to know me better. Of course I'm not cross. And of course you must tour with Valdès. I shall be all right. How do you suppose I managed before I invented you?' I smiled like an indulgent mother.

'Oh! I didn't mean that,' she said. 'I know you're frightfully clever. I'm nothing——'

'I hope you'll be awfully happy,' I whispered, squeezing her hand. 'And don't forget that I introduced him to you—I knew him years before you did. I'm the cause of this bliss——Do you remember that cold morning in Berlin?'

'Oh! well, I should say!' she exclaimed in ecstasy.

When we reached our rooms in the hotel I kissed her warmly. Women do that sort of thing.

Then a card was brought to me. 'George Capey,' it said; and in pencil, 'Of the Five Towns.'

I shrugged my shoulders. Sally had gone to scribble a note to her Valdès. 'Show Mr. Capey in,' I said, and a natty young man entered, half nervousness, half audacity.

'How did you know I come from the Five Towns?' I questioned him.

'I am on the *Evening Mail*,' he said, 'where they know everything, madam.'

I was annoyed. 'Then they know, on the *Evening Mail* that Paquita Qita has never been interviewed, and never will be,' I said.

'Besides,' he went on, 'I come from the Five Towns myself.'

'Bursley?' I asked mechanically.

'Bursley,' he ejaculated; then added, 'you haven't been near old Bosley since——'

It was true.

'No,' I said hastily. 'It is many years since I have been in England, even. Do they know down there who Qita is?'

'Not they!' he replied.

I grew reflective. Stars such as I have no place of origin. We shoot up out of a void, and sink back into a void. I had forgotten Bursley and Bursley folk. Recollections rushed in upon me.... I felt beautifully sad. I drew off my gloves, and flung my hat on a chair with a movement that would have bewitched a man of the world, but Mr. George Capey was unimpressed. I laughed.

'What's the joke?' he inquired. I adored him for his Bursliness.

'I was just thinking, of fat Mrs. Cartledge, who used to keep that fishmonger's shop in Oldcastle Street, opposite Bates's. I wonder if she's still there?'

'She is,' he said. 'And fatter than ever! She's getting on in years now.'

I broke the rule of a lifetime, and let him interview me.

'Tell them I'm thirty-seven,' I said. 'Yes, I mean it. Tell them.'

And then for another tit-bit I explained to him how I had discovered Sally at Koster and Bial's, in New York, five years ago, and made her my sister for stage purposes because I was lonely, and liked her American simplicity and twang. He departed full of tea and satisfaction.

It was our last night at the Aquarium. The place was crammed. The houses where I performed were always crammed. Our turn was in three parts, and lasted half an hour. The first part was a skirt dance in full afternoon dress (*danse de modernité*, I called it); the second was a double horizontal bar act; the third was the famous act of the red and the blue ropes, in full evening dress. It was 10.45 when we climbed the silk ladders for the third part. High up in the roof, separated from each other by nearly the length of the great hall, Sally and I stood on two little platforms. I held the ends of the red and the blue ropes. I had to let the blue rope swing across the hall to her. She would seize it, and, clutching it, swoop like the ball of an enormous pendulum from her platform to mine. (But would she?) I should then swing on the red rope to the platform she had left.

Then the band would stop for the thrilling moment, and the lights would be lowered. Each lighting and holding a powerful electric hand-light—one red, one blue—we should signal the drummer and plunge simultaneously into space, flash past each other in mid-flight, exchanging lights as we passed (this was the trick), and soar to opposite platforms again, amid frenzied applause. There were no nets.

That was what ought to occur.

I stood bowing to the floor of tiny upturned heads, and jerking the ropes a little. Then I let Sally's rope go with a push, and it dropped away from me, and in a few seconds she had it safe in her strong hand. She was taller than me, with a fuller figure, yet she looked quite small on her distant platform. All the evening I had been thinking of fat old Mrs. Cartledge messing and slopping among cod and halibut on white tiles. I could not get Bursley and my silly infancy out of my head. I followed my feverish career from the age of fifteen, when that strange Something in me, which makes an artist, had first driven me forth to conquer two continents. I thought of all the golden loves I had scorned, and my own love, which had been ignored, unnoticed, but which still obstinately burned. I glanced downwards and descried Valdès precisely where Sally had said he would be. Valdès, what a fool you were! And I hated a fool. I am one of those who can love and hate, who can love and despise, who can love and loathe the same object in the same moment. Then I signalled to Sally to plunge, and my eyes filled with tears. For, you see, somehow, in some senseless sentimental way, the thought of fat Mrs. Cartledge and my silly infancy had forced me to send Sally the red rope, not the blue one. We exchanged ropes on alternate nights, but this was her night for the blue one.

She swung over, alighting accurately at my side with that exquisite outward curve of the spine which had originally attracted me to her.

'You sent me the red one,' she said to me, after she had acknowledged the applause.

'Yes,' I said. 'Never mind; stick to it now you've got it. Here's the red light. Have you seen Valdès?'

She nodded.

I took the blue light and clutched the blue rope. Instead of murder—suicide, since it must be one or the other. And why not? Indeed, I censured myself in that second for having meant to kill Sally. Not because I was ashamed of the sin, but because the revenge would have been so pitiful and weak. If Valdès the matchless was capable of passing me over and kneeling to the pretty thing——

I stood ready. The world was to lose that fineness, that distinction, that originality, that disturbing subtlety, which constituted Paquita Qita. I plunged.

... I was on the other platform. The rope had held, then: I remembered nothing of the flight except that I had passed near the upturned, pleasant face of Valdès.

The band stopped. The lights of the hall were lowered. All was dark. I switched on my dazzling blue light; Sally switched on her red one. I stood ready. The rope could not possibly endure a second strain. I waved to Sally and signalled to the conductor. The world was to lose Paquita. The drum began its formidable roll. Whirrr! I plunged, and saw the red star rushing towards me. I snatched it and soared upwards. The blue rope seemed to tremble. As I came near the platform at decreasing speed, it seemed to stretch like elastic. It broke! The platform jumped up suddenly over my head, but I caught at the silk ladder. I was saved! There was a fearful silence, and then the appalling shock of hysterical applause from seven thousand throats. I slid down the ladder, ran across the stage into my dressing-room for a cloak, out again into the street. In two days I was in Buda-Pesth.

NOCTURNE AT THE MAJESTIC

I

In the daily strenuous life of a great hotel there are periods during which its bewildering activities slacken, and the vast organism seems to be under the influence of an opiate. Such a period recurs after dinner when the guests are preoccupied by the mysterious processes of digestion in the drawing-rooms or smoking-rooms or in the stalls of a theatre. On the evening of this nocturne the well-known circular entrance-hall of the Majestic, with its tessellated pavement, its malachite pillars, its Persian rugs, its lounges, and its renowned stuffed bears at the foot of the grand stairway, was for the moment deserted, save by the head hall-porter and the head night-porter and the girl in the bureau. It was a quarter to nine, and the head hall-porter was abdicating his pagoda to the head night-porter, and telling him the necessary secrets of the day. These two lords, before whom the motley panorama of human existence was continually being enrolled, held a portentous confabulation night and morning. They had no illusions; they knew life. Shakespeare himself might have listened to them with advantage.

The girl in the bureau, like a beautiful and languishing animal in its cage, leaned against her window, and looked between two pillars at the magnificent lords. She was too far off to catch their talk, and, indeed, she watched them absently in a reverie induced by the sweet melancholy of the summer twilight, by the torpidity of the hour, and by the prospect of the next day, which was her day off. The liveried functionaries ignored her, probably scorned her as a mere pretty little morsel. Nevertheless, she was the centre of energy, not they. If money were payable, she was the person to receive it; if a customer wanted a room, she would choose it; and the lords had to call her 'miss.' The immense and splendid hotel pulsed round this simple heart hidden under a white blouse. Especially in summer, her presence and the presence of her companions in the bureau (but to-night she was alone) ministered to the satisfaction of male guests, whose cruel but profoundly human instincts found pleasure in the fact that, no matter when they came in from their wanderings, the pretty captives were always there in the bureau, smiling welcome, puzzling stupid little brains and puckering pale brows over enormous ledgers, twittering borrowed facetiousness from rosy mouths, and smoothing out seductive toilettes with long thin hands that were made for ring and bracelet and rudder-lines, and not a bit for the pen and the ruler.

The pretty little thing despised of the functionaries corresponded almost exactly in appearance to the typical bureau girl. She was moderately tall; she had a good slim figure, all pleasant curves, flaxen hair and plenty of it, and a dainty, rather expressionless face; the ears and mouth were very small, the eyes large and blue, the nose so-so, the cheeks and forehead of an equal ivory pallor, the chin trifling, with a crease under the lower lip and a rich convexity springing out from below the crease. The extremities of the full lips were nearly always drawn up in a smile, mechanical, but infallibly attractive. The hair was of an orthodox frizziness.

You would have said she was a nice, kind, good-natured girl, flirtatious but correct, well adapted to adorn a dogcart on Sundays.

This was Nina, foolish Nina, aged twenty-one. In her reverie the entire Hôtel Majestic weighed on her; she had a more than adequate sense of her own solitary importance in the bureau, and stirring obscurely beneath that consciousness were the deep ineradicable longings of a poor pretty girl for heaps of money, endless luxury of finery and chocolates, and sentimental silken dalliance.

Suddenly a stranger entered the hall. His advent seemed to wake the place out of the trance into which it had fallen. The nocturne had begun. Nina straightened herself and intensified her eternal smile. The two porters became military, and smiled with a special and peculiar urbanity. Several lesser but still lordly functionaries appeared among the pillars; a page-boy emerged by magic from the region of the chimney-piece like Mephistopheles in Faust's study; and some guests of both sexes strolled chattering across the tessellated pavement as they passed from one wing of the hotel to the other.

'How do, Tom?' said the stranger, grasping the hand of the head hall-porter, and nodding to the head night-porter.

His voice showed that he was an American, and his demeanour that he was one of those experienced, wealthy, and kindly travellers who know the Christian names of all the hall-porters in the world, and have the trick of securing their intimacy and fealty. He wore a blue suit and a light gray wideawake, and his fine moustache was grizzled. In his left hand he carried a brown bag.

'Nicely, thank you, sir,' Tom replied. 'How are you, sir?'

'Oh, about six and six.'

Whereupon both porters laughed heartily.

Tom escorted him to the bureau, and tried to relieve him of his bag. Inferior lords escorted Tom.

'I guess I'll keep the grip,' said the stranger. 'Mr. Pank will be around with some more baggage pretty soon. We've expressed the rest on to the steamer. Well, my dear,' he went on, turning to Nina, 'you're a fresh face here.'

He looked her steadily in the eyes.

'Yes, I am,' she said, conquered instantly.

Radiant and triumphant, the man brought good-humour into every face, like some wonderful combination of the sun and the sea-breeze.

'Give me two bedrooms and a parlour, please,' he commanded.

'First floor?' asked Nina prettily.

'First floor! Well—I should say! *And* on the Strand, my dear.'

She bent over her ledgers, blushing.

'Send someone to the 'phone, Tom, and let 'em put me on to the Regency, will you?' said the stranger.

'Yes, sir. Samuels, go and ring up the Regency Theatre—quick!'

Swift departure of a lord.

'And ask Alphonse to come up to my bedroom in ten minutes from now,' the stranger proceeded to Tom. 'I shall want a dandy supper for fourteen at a quarter after eleven.'

'Yes, sir. No dinner, sir?'

'No; we dined on the Pullman. Well, my dear, figured it out yet?'

'Numbers 102, 120, and 107,' said Nina.

'Keys 102, 120, and 107,' said Tom.

Swift departure of another lord to the pagoda.

'How much?' demanded the stranger.

'The bedrooms are twenty-five shillings, and the sitting-room two guineas.'

'I guess Mr. Pank won't mind that. Hullo, Pank, you're here! I'm through. Your number's 102 or 120, which you fancy. Just going to the 'phone a minute, and then I'll join you upstairs.'

Mr. Pank was a younger man, possessing a thin, astute, intellectual face. He walked into the hall with noticeable deliberation. His travelling costume was faultless, but from beneath his straw hat his black hair sprouted in a somewhat peculiar fashion over his broad forehead. He smiled lazily and shrewdly, and without a word disappeared into a lift. Two large portmanteaus accompanied him.

Presently the elder stranger could be heard battling with the obstinate idiosyncrasies of a London telephone.

'You haven't registered,' Nina called to him in her tremulous, delicate, captivating voice, as he came out of the telephone-box.

He advanced to sign, and, taking a pen and leaning on the front of the bureau, wrote in the visitor's book, in a careful, legible hand: 'Lionel Belmont, New York.' Having thus written, and still resting on the right elbow, he raised his right hand a little and waved the pen like a delicious menace at Nina.

'Mr. Pank hasn't registered, either,' he said slowly, with a charming affectation of solemnity, as though accusing Mr. Pank of some appalling crime.

Nina laughed timidly as she pushed his room-ticket across the page of the big book. She thought that Mr. Lionel Belmont was perfectly delightful.

'No,' he hasn't,' she said, trying also to be arch; 'but he must.'

At that moment she happened to glance at the right hand of Mr. Belmont. In the brilliance of the electric light she could see the fair skin of the wrist and forearm within the whiteness of his shirt-sleeve. She stared at what she saw, every muscle tense.

'I guess you can round up Mr. Pank yourself, my dear, later on,' said Lionel Belmont, and turned quickly away, intent on the next thing.

He did not notice that her large eyes had grown larger and her pale face paler. In another moment the hall was deserted again. Mr. Belmont had ascended in the lift, Tom had gone to his rest, and the head night-porter was concealed in the pagoda. Nina sank down limply on her stool, her nostrils twitching; she feared she was about to faint, but this final calamity did not occur. She had, nevertheless, experienced the greatest shock of her brief life, and the way of it was thus.

II

Nina Malpas was born amid the embers of one of those fiery conjugal dramas which occur with romantic frequency in the provincial towns of the northern Midlands, where industrial conditions are such as to foster an independent spirit among women of the lower class generally, and where by long tradition 'character' is allowed to exploit itself more freely than in the southern parts of our island. Lemuel Malpas was a dashing young commercial traveller, with what is known as 'an agreeable address,' in Bursley, one of the Five Towns, Staffordshire. On the strength of his dash he wooed and married the daughter of an hotel-keeper in the neighbouring town of Hanbridge. Six months after the wedding—in other words, at the most dangerous period of the connubial career—Mrs. Malpas's father died, and Mrs. Malpas became the absolute mistress of eight thousand pounds. Lemuel[1] had carefully foreseen this windfall, and wished to use the money in enterprises of the earthenware trade. Mrs. Malpas, pretty and vivacious, with a self-conceit hardened by the adulation of saloon-bars, very decidedly thought otherwise. Her motto was, 'What's yours is mine, but what's mine's my own.' The difference was accentuated. Long mutual resistances were followed by reconciliations, which grew more and more transitory, and at length both recognised that the union, not founded on genuine affection, had been a mistake.

[1] This name is pronounced with the accent on the first syllable in the Five Towns.

'Keep your d——d brass!' Lemuel exclaimed one morning, and he went off on a journey and forgot to come back. A curious letter dated from Liverpool wished his wife happiness, and informed her that, since she was well provided for, he had no scruples about leaving her. Mrs. Malpas was startled at first, but she soon perceived that what Lemuel had done was exactly what the brilliant and enterprising Lemuel might have been expected to do. She jerked up her doll's head, and ejaculated, 'So much the better!'

A few weeks later she sold the furniture and took rooms in Scarborough, where, amid pleasurable surroundings, she determined to lead the joyous life of a grass-widow, free of all cares. Then, to her astonishment and disgust, Nina was born. She had not bargained for Nina. She found herself in the tiresome position of a mother whose explanations of her child lack plausibility. One lodging-housekeeper to whom she hazarded the statement that Lemuel was in Australia had saucily replied: 'I thought maybe it was the North Pole he was gone to!'

This decided Mrs. Malpas. She returned suddenly to the Five Towns, where at least her reputation was secure. Only a week previously Lemuel had learnt indirectly that she had left their native district. He determined thenceforward to forget her completely. Mrs. Malpas's prettiness was of the fleeting sort. After Nina's birth she began to get stout and coarse, and the nostalgia of the saloon-bar, the coffee-room, and the sanded portico overtook her. The Tiger at Bursley was for sale, a respectable commercial hotel, the best in the town. She purchased it, wines, omnibus connection, and all, and developed into the typical landlady in black silk and gold rings.

In the Tiger Nina was brought up. She was a pretty child from her earliest years, and received the caresses of all as a matter of course. She went to a good school, studied the piano, and learnt dancing, and at sixteen did her hair up. She did as she was told without fuss, being apparently of a lethargic temperament; she had all the money and all the clothes that her heart could desire; she was happy, and in a quiet way she deemed herself a rather considerable item in the world. When she was eighteen her mother died miserably of cancer, and it was discovered that the liabilities of Mrs. Malpas's estate exceeded its assets—and the Tiger mortgaged up to its value! The creditors were not angry; they attributed the state of affairs to illness and the absence of male control, and good-humouredly accepted what they could get. None the less, Nina, the child of luxury and sloth, had to start life with several hundreds of pounds less than nothing. Of her father all trace had been long since lost. A place was found for her, and for over two years she saw the world from the office of a famous hotel in Doncaster. Her lethargy, and an invaluable gift of adapting herself to circumstances, saved her from any acute unhappiness in the Yorkshire town. Instinctively she ceased to remember the Tiger and past splendours. (Equally, if she had married a Duke instead of becoming a book-keeper, she would have ceased to remember the Tiger and past humility.) Then by good or ill fortune she had the offer of a situation at the Hôtel Majestic, Strand, London. The Majestic and the sights thereof woke up the sleeping soul.

Before her death Mrs. Malpas had told Nina many things about the vanished Lemuel; among others, the curious detail that he had two small moles—one hairless, the other hirsute—close together on the under side of his right wrist. Nina had seen precisely such marks of identification on the right wrist of Mr. Lionel Belmont.

She was convinced that Lionel Belmont was her father. There could not be two men in the world so stamped by nature. She perceived that in changing his name he had chosen Lionel because of its similarity to Lemuel. She felt certain, too, that she had noticed vestiges of the Five Towns accent beneath his Americanisms. But apart from these reasons, she knew by a superrational instinct that Lionel Belmont was her father; it was not the call of blood, but the positiveness of a woman asserting that a thing is so because she is sure it is so.

III

Nina was not of an imaginative disposition. The romance of this extraordinary encounter made no appeal to her. She was the sort of girl that constantly reads novelettes, and yet always, with fatigued scorn, refers to them as 'silly.' Stupid little Nina was intensely practical at heart, and it was the practical side of her father's reappearance that engaged her birdlike mind. She did not stop to reflect that truth is stranger than fiction. Her tiny heart was not agitated by any ecstatic ponderings upon the wonder and mystery of fate. She did not feel strangely drawn towards Lionel Belmont, nor did she feel that he supplied a something which had always been wanting to her.

On the other hand, her pride—and Nina was very proud—found much satisfaction in the fact that her father, having turned up, was so fine, handsome, dashing, good-humoured, and wealthy. It was well, and excellently well, and delicious, to have a father like that. The possession of such a father opened up vistas of a future so enticing and glorious that her present career became instantly loathsome to her.

It suddenly seemed impossible that she could have tolerated the existence of a hotel clerk for a single week. Her eyes were opened, and she saw, as many women have seen, that luxury was an absolute necessity to her. All her ideas soared with the magic swiftness of the bean-stalk. And at the same time she was terribly afraid, unaccountably afraid, to confront Mr. Belmont and tell him that she was his Nina; he was entirely unaware that he had a Nina.

'I'm your daughter! I know by your moles!'

She whispered the words in her tiny heart, and felt sure that she could never find courage to say them aloud to that great and important man. The announcement would be too monstrous, incredible, and absurd. People would laugh. He would laugh. And Nina could stand anything better than being laughed at. Even supposing she proved to him his paternity—she thought of the horridness of going to lawyers' offices—he might decline to recognise her. Or he might throw her fifty pounds a year, as one throws sixpence to an importunate crossing-sweeper, to be rid of her. The United States existed in her mind chiefly as a country of highly-remarkable divorce laws, and she thought that Mr. Belmont might have married again. A fashionable and arrogant Mrs. Belmont, and a dazzling Miss Belmont, aged possibly eighteen, might arrive, both of them steeped in all conceivable luxury, at any moment. Where would Nina be then, with her two-and-eleven-pence-halfpenny blouse from Glave's?...

Mr. Belmont, accompanied by Alphonse, the head-waiter in the *salle à manger*, descended in the lift and crossed the hall to the portico, where he stood talking for a few seconds. Mr. Belmont turned, and, as he conversed with Alphonse, gazed absently in the direction of the bureau. He looked straight through the pretty captive. After all, despite his superficial heartiness, she could be nothing to him—so rich, assertive, and truly important. A hansom was called for him, and he departed; she observed that he was in evening dress now.

No! Her cause was just; but it was too startling—that was what was the matter with it.

Then she told herself she would write to Lionel Belmont. She would write a letter that night.

At nine-thirty she was off duty. She went upstairs to her perch in the roof, and sat on her bed for over two hours. Then she came down again to the bureau with some bluish note-paper and envelopes in her hand, and, in response to the surprised question of the pink-frocked colleague who had taken her place, she explained that she wanted to write a letter.

'You do look that bad, Miss Malpas,' said the other girl, who made a speciality of compassion.

'Do I?' said Nina.

'Yes, you do. What have you got *on*, *now*, my poor dear?'

'What's that to you? I'll thank you to mind your own business, Miss Bella Perkins.'

Usually Nina was not soon ruffled; but that night all her nerves were exasperated and exceedingly sensitive.

'Oh!' said the girl. 'What price the Duchess of Doncaster? And I was just going to wish you a nice day to-morrow for your holiday, too.'

Nina seated herself at the table to write the letter. An electric light burned directly over her frizzy head. She wrote a weak but legible and regular back-hand. She hated writing letters, partly because she was dubious about her spelling, and partly because of an obscure but irrepressible suspicion that her letters were of necessity silly. She pondered for a long time, and then wrote: 'Dear Mr. Belmont,—I venture——' She made a new start: 'Dear Sir,—I hope you will not think me——' And a third attempt: 'My dear Father——' No! it was preposterous. It could no more be written than it could be said.

The situation was too much for simple Nina.

Suddenly the grand circular hall of the Majestic was filled with a clamour at once charming and fantastic. There was chattering of musical, gay American voices, pattering of elegant feet on the tessellated pavement, the unique incomparable sound of the *frou-frou* of many frocks; and above all this the rich tones of Mr. Lionel Belmont. Nina looked up and saw her radiant father the centre of a group of girls all young, all beautiful, all stylish, all with picture hats, all self-possessed, all sparkling, doubtless the recipients of the dandy supper.

Oh, how insignificant and homicidal Nina felt!

'Thirteen of you!' exclaimed Lionel Belmont, pulling his superb moustache. 'Two to a hansom. I guess I'll want six and a half hansoms, boy.'

There was an explosion of delicious laughter, and the page-boy grinned, ran off, and began whistling in the portico like a vexed locomotive. The thirteen fair, shepherded by Lionel Belmont, passed out into the murmurous summer night of the Strand. Cab after cab drove up, and Nina saw that her father, after filling each cab, paid each cabman. In three minutes the dream-like scene was over. Mr. Belmont re-entered the hotel, winked humorously at the occupant of the pagoda, ignored the bureau, and departed to his rooms.

Nina ripped her inchoate letters into small pieces, and, with a tart good-night to Miss Bella Perkins, who was closing her ledgers, the hour being close upon twelve-thirty, she passed sedately, stiffly, as though in performance of some vestal's ritual, up the grand staircase. Turning to the right at the first landing, she traversed a long corridor which was no part of the route to her cubicle on the ninth floor. This corridor was lighted by glowing sparks, which hung on yellow cords from the central line of the ceiling; underfoot was a heavy but narrow crimson patterned carpet with a strip of polished oak parquet on either side of it. Exactly along the central line of the carpet Nina tripped, languorously, like an automaton, and exactly over her head glittered the line of electric sparks. The corridor and the journey seemed to be interminable, and Nina on some inscrutable and mystic errand. At length she moved aside from the religious line, went into a service cabinet, and emerged with a small bunch of pass-keys. No. 107 was Lionel Belmont's sitting-room; No. 102, his bedroom, was opposite to 107. No. 108, another sitting-room, was, as Nina knew, unoccupied. She noiselessly let herself into No. 108, closed the door, and stood still. After a minute she switched on the light. These two rooms, Nos. 108 and 107, had once communicated, but, as space grew precious with the growing success of the Majestic, they had been finally separated, and the door between them locked and masked by furniture. By reason of the door, Nina could hear Lionel Belmont moving to and fro in No. 107. She listened a long time. Then, involuntarily, she yawned with fatigue.

'How silly of me to be here!' she thought. 'What good will this do me?'

She extinguished the light and opened the door to leave. At the same instant the door of No. 107, three feet off, opened. She drew back with a start of horror. Suppose she had collided with her father on the landing! Timorously she peeped out, and saw Lionel Belmont, in his shirt-sleeves, disappear round the corner.

'He is going to talk with his friend Mr. Pank,' Nina thought, knowing that No. 120 lay at some little distance round that corner.

Mr. Belmont had left the door of No. 107 slightly ajar. An unseen and terrifying force compelled Nina to venture into the corridor, and then to push the door of No. 107 wide open. The same force, not at all herself, quite beyond herself, seemed to impel her by the shoulders into the room. As she stood unmistakably within her father's private sitting-room, scared, breathing rapidly, inquisitive, she said to herself:

'I shall hear him coming back, and I can run out before he turns the corner of the corridor.' And she kept her little pink ears alert.

She looked about the softly brilliant room, such an extravagant triumph of luxurious comfort as twenty years ago would have aroused comment even in Mayfair; but there were scores of similar rooms in the Majestic. No one thought twice of them. Her father's dress-coat was thrown arrogantly over a Louis Quatorze chair, and this careless flinging of the expensive shining coat across the gilded chair somehow gave Nina a more intimate appreciation of her father's grandeur and of the great and glorious life he led. She longed to recline indolently in a priceless tea-gown on the couch by the fireplace and issue orders.... She approached the writing-table, littered with papers, documents, in scores and hundreds. To the left was the brown bag. It was locked, and very heavy, she thought. To the right was a pile of telegrams. She picked up one, and read:

'*Pank, Grand Hotel, Birmingham. Why not burgle hotel? Simplest most effective plan and solves all difficulties.—BELMONT.*'

She read it twice, crunched it in her left hand, and picked up another one:

'Pank, Adelphi Hotel, Liverpool. Your objection absurd. See safe in bureau at Majestic. Quite easy. Scene with girl second evening.—BELMONT.'

The thing flashed blindingly upon her. Her father and Mr. Pank belonged to the swell mob of which she had heard and seen so much at Doncaster. She at once became the excessively knowing and suspicious hotel employé, to whom every stranger is a rogue until he has proved the contrary. Had she lived through three St. Leger weeks for nothing? At the hotel at Doncaster, what they didn't know about thieves and sharpers was not knowledge. The landlord kept a loaded revolver in his desk there during the week. And she herself had been provided with a whistle which she was to blow at the slightest sign of a row; she had blown it once, and seven policemen had appeared within thirty seconds. The landlord used to tell tales of masterly and huge scoundrelism that would make Charles Peace turn in his grave. And the landlord had ever insisted that no one, no one at all, could always distinguish with certainty between a real gent and a swell-mobsman.

So her father and Mr. Pank had deceived everyone in the hotel except herself, and they meant to rob the safe in the bureau to-morrow night. Of course Mr. Lionel Belmont was a villain, or he would not have deserted her poor dear mother; it was annoying, but indubitable.... Even now he was maturing his plans round the corner with that Mr. Pank.... Burglars always went about in shirt-sleeves.... The brown bag contained the tools....

The shock was frightful, disastrous, tragic; but it had solved the situation by destroying it. Practically, Nina no longer had a father. He had existed for about four hours as a magnificent reality, full of possibilities; he now ceased to be recognisable.

She was about to pick up a third telegram when a slight noise caused her to turn swiftly; she had forgotten to keep her little pink ears alert. Her father stood in the doorway. He was certainly the victim of some extraordinary emotion; his face worked; he seemed at a loss what to do or say; he seemed pained, confused, even astounded. Simple, foolish Nina had upset the balance of his equations.

Then he resumed his self-control and came forward into the room with a smile intended to be airy. Meanwhile Nina had not moved. One is inclined to pity the artless and defenceless girl in this midnight duel of wits with a shrewd, resourceful, and unscrupulous man of the world. But one's pity should not be lavished on an undeserving object. Though Nina trembled, she was mistress of herself. She knew just where she was, and just how to behave. She was as impregnable as Gibraltar.

'Well,' said Mr. Lionel Belmont, genially gazing at her pose, 'you do put snap into it, any way.'

'Into what?' she was about to inquire, but prudently she held her tongue. Drawing, herself up with the gesture of an offended and unapproachable queen, the little thing sailed past him, close past her own father, and so out of the room.

'Say!' she heard him remark: 'let's straighten this thing out, eh?'

But she heroically ignored him, thinking the while that, with all his sins, he was attractive enough. She still held the first telegram in her long, thin fingers.

So ended the nocturne.

IV

At five o'clock the next morning Nina's trifling nose was pressed against the windowpane of her cubicle. In the enormous slate roof of the Majestic are three rows of round windows, like port-holes. Out of the highest one, at the extremity of the left wing, Nina looked. From thence she could see five other vast hotels, and the yard of Charing Cross Station, with three night-cabs drawn up to the kerb, and a red van of W.H. Smith and Son disappearing into the station. The Strand was quite empty. It was a strange world of sleep and grayness and disillusion. Within a couple of hundred yards or so of her thousands of people lay asleep, and they would all soon wake into the disillusion, and the Strand would wake, and the first omnibus of all the omnibuses would come along....

Never had simple Nina felt so sad and weary. She was determined to give up her father. She was bound to tell the manager of her discovery, for Nina was an honest servant, and she was piqued in her honesty. No one should know that Lionel Belmont was her father.... She saw before her the task of forgetting him and forgetting the rich dreams of which he had been the origin. She was once more a book-keeper with no prospects.

At eight she saw the manager in the managerial room. Mr. Reuben was a young Jew, aged about thirty-four, with a cold but indestructibly polite manner. He was a great man, and knew it; he had almost invented the Majestic.

She told him her news; it was impossible for foolish Nina to conceal her righteousness and her sense of her importance.

'Whom did you say, Miss Malpas?' asked Mr. Reuben.

'Mr. Lionel Belmont—at least, that's what he calls himself.'

'Calls himself, Miss Malpas?'

'Here's one of the telegrams.'

Mr. Reuben read it, looked at little Nina, and smiled; he never laughed.

'Is it possible, Miss Malpas,' said he, 'that you don't know who Mr. Belmont and Mr. Pank are?' And then, as she shook her head, he continued in his impassive, precise way: 'Mr. Belmont is one of the principal theatrical managers in the United States. Mr. Pank is one of the principal playwrights in the United States. Mr. Pank's melodrama 'Nebraska' is now being played at the Regency by Mr. Belmont's own American company. Another of Mr. Belmont's companies starts shortly for a tour in the provinces with the musical comedy 'The Dolmenico Doll.' I believe that Mr. Pank and Mr. Belmont are now writing a new melodrama, and as they have both been travelling, but not together, I expect that these telegrams relate to that melodrama. Did you suppose that safe-burglars wire their plans to each other like this?' He waved the telegram with a gesture of fatigue.

Silly, ruined Nina made no answer.

'Do you ever read the papers—the *Telegraph* or the *Mail*, Miss Malpas?'

'N-no, sir.'

'You ought to, then you wouldn't be so ignorant and silly. A hotel-clerk can't know too much. And, by-the-way, what were you doing in Mr. Belmont's room last night, when you found these wonderful telegrams?'

'I went there—I went there—to——'

'Don't cry, please, it won't help you. You must leave here to-day. You've been here three weeks, I think. I'll tell Mr. Smith to pay you your month's wages. You don't know enough for the Majestic, Miss Malpas. Or perhaps you know too much. I'm sorry. I had thought you would suit us. Keep straight, that's all I have to say to you. Go back to Doncaster, or wherever it is you came from. Leave before five o'clock. That will do.'

With a godlike air, Mr. Reuben swung round his office-chair and faced his desk. He tried not to perceive that there was a mysterious quality about this case which he had not quite understood. Nina tripped piteously out.

In the whole of London Nina had one acquaintance, and an hour or so later, after drinking some tea, she set forth to visit this acquaintance. The weight of her own foolishness, fatuity, silliness, and ignorance was heavy upon her. And, moreover, she had been told that Mr. Lionel Belmont had already departed back to America, his luggage being marked for the American Transport Line.

She was primly walking, the superlative of the miserable, past the façade of the hotel, when someone sprang out of a cab and spoke to her. And it was Mr. Lionel Belmont.

'Get right into this hansom, Miss Malpas,' he said kindly, 'and I guess we'll talk it out.'

'Talk what out?' she thought.

But she got in.

'Marble Arch, and go up Regent Street, and don't hurry,' said Mr. Belmont to the cabman.

'How did he know my name?' she asked herself.

'A hansom's the most private place in London,' he said after a pause.

It certainly did seem to her very cosy and private, and her nearness to one of the principal theatrical managers in America was almost startling. Her white frock, with the black velvet decorations, touched his gray suit.

'Now,' he said, 'I do wish you'd tell me why you were in my parlour last night. Honest.'

'What for?' she parried, to gain time.

Should she begin to disclose her identity?

'Because—well, because—oh, look here, my girl, I want to be on very peculiar terms with you. I want to straighten out everything. You'll be sort of struck, but I'll be bound to tell you I'm your father. Now, don't faint or anything.'

'Oh, I knew that!' she gasped. 'I saw the moles on your wrist when your were registering—mother told me about them. Oh, if I had only known you knew!'

They looked at one another.

'It was only the day before yesterday I found out I possessed such a thing as a daughter. I had a kind of fancy to go around to the old spot. This notion of me having a daughter struck me considerable, and I concluded to trace her and size her up at once.' Nina was bound to smile. 'So your poor mother's been dead three years?'

'Yes,' said Nina.

'Ah! don't let us talk about that. I feel I can't say just the right thing.... And so you knew me by those pips.' He pulled up his right sleeve. 'Was that why you came up to my parlour?'

Nina nodded, and Lionel Belmont sighed with relief.

'Why didn't you tell me at once, my dear, who you where?'

'I didn't dare,' she smiled; 'I was afraid. I thought you wouldn't——'

'Listen,' he said; 'I've wanted someone like you for years, years, and years. I've got no one to look after——'

'Then why didn't *you* tell *me* at once who you were?' she questioned with adorable pertness.

'Oh!' he laughed; 'how could I—plump like that? When I saw you first, in the bureau, the stricken image of your mother at your age, I was nearly down. But I came up all right, didn't I, my dear? I acted it out well, didn't I?'

The hansom was rolling through Hyde Park, and the sunshiny hour was eleven in June. Nina looked forth on the gay and brilliant scene: rhododendrons, duchesses, horses, dandies—the incomparable wealth and splendour of the capital. She took a long breath, and began to be happy for the rest of her life. She felt that, despite her plain frock, she was in this picture. Her father had told her that his income was rising on a hundred and fifty thousand dollars a year, and he would thank her to spend it. Her father had told her, when she had confessed the scene with Mr. Reuben and what led to it, that she had grit, and that the mistake was excusable, and that a girl as pretty as she was didn't want to be as fly as Mr. Reuben had said. Her father had told her that he was proud of her, and he had not been so rude as to laugh at her blunder.

She felt that she was about to enter upon the true and only vocation of a dainty little morsel—namely, to spend money earned by other people. She thought less homicidally now of the thirteen chorus-girls of the previous night.

'Say,' said her father, 'I sail this afternoon for New York, Nina.'

'They said you'd gone, at the hotel.'

'Only my baggage. The *Minnehaha* clears at five. I guess I want you to come along too. On the voyage we'll get acquainted, and tell each other things.'

'Suppose I say I won't?'

She spoke despotically, as the pampered darling should.

'Then I'll wait for the next boat. But it'll be awkward.'

'Then I'll come. But I've got no things.'

He pushed up the trap-door.

Driver, Bond Street. And get on to yourself, for goodness' sake! Hurry!'

'You told me not to hurry,' grumbled the cabby.

'And now I tell you to hustle. See?'

'Shall you want me to call myself Belmont?' Nina asked.

'I chose it because it was a fine ten-horse-power name twenty years ago,' said her father; and she murmured that she liked the name very much.

As Lionel Belmont the Magnificent paid the cabman, and Nina walked across the pavement into one of the most famous repositories of expensive frippery in the world, she thrilled with the profoundest pleasure her tiny soul was capable of. Foolish, simple Nina had achieved the *nec plus ultra* of her languorous dreams.

CLARICE OF THE AUTUMN CONCERTS

I

'What did you say your name was?' asked Otto, the famous concert manager.
'Clara Toft.'

'That won't do,' he said roughly.

'My real proper name is Clarice,' she added, blushing. 'But——'

'That's better, that's better.' His large, dark face smiled carelessly. 'Clarice—
and stick an "e" on to Toft—Clarice Tofte. Looks like either French or German
then. I'll send you the date. It'll be the second week in September. And you can
come round to the theatre and try the piano—Bechstein.'

'And what do you think I had better play, Mr. Otto?'

'You must play what you have just played, of course. Tschaikowsky's all the
rage just now. Your left hand's very weak, especially in the last movement. You've
got to make more noise—at my concerts. And see here, Miss Toft, don't you go
and make a fool of me. I believe you have a great future, and I'm backing my
opinion. Don't you go and make a fool of me.'

'I shall play my very best,' she smiled nervously. 'I'm awfully obliged to you,
Mr. Otto.'

'Well,' he said, 'you ought to be.'

At the age of fifteen her father, an earthenware manufacturer, and the
flamboyant Alderman of Turnhill, in the Five Towns, had let her depart to
London to the Royal College of Music. Thence, at nineteen, she had proceeded to
the Conservatoire of Liége. At twenty-two she could play the great concert
pieces—Liszt's 'Rhapsodies Hongroises,' Chopin's Ballade, Op. 47, Beethoven's
Op. 111, etc.—in concert style, and she was the wonder of the Five Towns when
she visited Turnhill. But in London she had obtained neither engagements nor
pupils: she had never believed in herself. She knew of dozens of pianists whom
she deemed more brilliant than little, pretty, modest Clara Toft; and after her
father's death and the not surprising revelation of his true financial condition, she
settled with her faded, captious mother in Turnhill as a teacher of the pianoforte,
and did nicely.

Then, when she was twenty-six, and content in provincialism, she had met
during an August holiday at Llandudno her old fellow pupil, Albert Barbellion,
who was conducting the Pier concerts. Barbellion had asked her to play at a
'soirée musicale' which he gave one night in the ball-room of his hotel, and she
had performed Tschaikowsky's immense and lurid Slavonic Sonata; and the
unparalleled Otto, renowned throughout the British Empire for Otto's Bohemian
Autumn Nightly Concerts at Covent Garden Theatre, had happened to hear her
and that seldom played sonata for the first time. It was a wondrous chance. Otto's
large, picturesque, extempore way of inviting her to appear at his promenade
concerts reminded her of her father.

II

In the bleak three-cornered artists'-room she could faintly hear the descending impetuous velocities of the Ride of the Walkyries. She was waiting in her new yellow dress, waiting painfully. Otto rushed in, a glass in his hand.

'You all right?' he questioned sharply.

'Oh, yes,' she said, getting up from the cane-chair.

'Let me see you stand on one leg,' he said; and then, because she hesitated: 'Go on, quick! Stand on one leg. It's a good test.' So she stood on one leg, foolishly smiling. 'Here, drink this,' he ordered, and she had to drink brandy-and-soda out of the glass. 'You're better now,' he remarked; and decidedly, though her throat tingled and she coughed, she felt equal to anything at that moment.

A stout, middle-aged woman, in a rather shabby opera cloak, entered the room.

'Ah, Cornelia!' exclaimed Otto grandly.

'My dear Otto!' the woman responded, wrinkling her wonderfully enamelled cheeks.

'Miss Toft, let me introduce you to Madame Lopez.' He turned to the newcomer. 'Keep her calm for me, bright star, will you?'

Then Otto went, and Clarice was left alone with the world-famous operatic soprano, who was advertised to sing that night the Shadow Song from 'Dinorah.'

'Where did he pick you up, my dear?' the decayed diva inquired maternally.

Clarice briefly explained.

'You aren't paying him anything, are you?'

'Oh, no!' said Clarice, shocked. 'But I get no fee this time——'

'Of course not, my dear,' the Lopez cut her short. 'It's all right so long as you aren't paying him anything to let you go on. Now run along.'

Clarice's heart stopped. The call-boy, with his cockney twang, had pronounced her name.

She moved forward, and, by dint of following the call-boy, at length reached the stage. Applause—good-natured applause—seemed to roll towards her from the uttermost parts of the vast auditorium. She realized with a start that this applause was exclusively for her. She sat down to the piano, and there ensued a death-like silence—a silence broken only by the striking of matches and the tinkle of the embowered fountain in front of the stage. She had a consciousness, rather than a vision, of a floor of thousands of upturned faces below her, and tier upon tier of faces rising above her and receding to the illimitable dark distances of the gallery. She heard a door bang, and perceived that some members of the orchestra were creeping quietly out at the back. Then she plunged, dizzy, into the sonata, as into a heaving and profound sea. The huge concert piano resounded under the onslaught of her broad hands. When she had played ten bars she knew with an absolute conviction that she would do justice to her talent. She could see, as it were, the entire sonata stretched out in detail before her like a road over which she had to travel....

At the end of the first movement the clapping enheartened her; she smiled confidently at the conductor, who, unemployed during her number, sat on a chair under his desk. Before recommencing she gazed boldly at the house, and certain placards—'Smoking permitted,' 'Emergency exit,' 'Ices,' and 'Fancy Dress Balls'—were fixed for ever on the retina of her eye. At the end of the second movement there was more applause, and the conductor tapped appreciation with his stick against the pillar of his desk; the leader of the listless orchestra also tapped with his fiddle-bow and nodded. It seemed to her now that she more and more dominated the piano, and that she rendered the great finale with masterful and fierce assurance....

She was pleased with herself as she banged the last massive chord. And the applause, the clapping, the hammering of sticks, astounded her, staggered her. She might have died of happiness while she bowed and bowed again. She ran off the stage triumphant, and the applause seemed to assail her little figure from all quarters and overwhelm it. As she stood waiting, concealed behind a group of palms, it suddenly occurred to her that, after all, she had underestimated herself. She saw her rosy future as the spoiled darling of continental capitals. The hail of clapping persisted, and the apparition of Otto violently waved her to return to the stage. She returned, bowed her passionate exultation with burning face and trembling knees, and retired. The clapping continued. Yes, she would be compelled to grant an encore—to *grant* one. She would grant it like a honeyed but imperious queen.

Suddenly she heard the warning tap of the conductor's baton; the applause was hushed as though by a charm, and the orchestra broke into the overture to 'Zampa.' She could not understand, she could not think. As she tripped tragically to the artists'-room in her new yellow dress she said to herself that the conductor must have made some mistake, and that——

'Very nice, my dear,' said the Lopez kindly to her. 'You got quite a call—quite a call.'

She waited for Otto to come and talk to her.

At length the Lopez was summoned, and Clarice followed to listen to her. And when the Lopez had soared with strong practised flight through the brilliant intricacy of the Shadow Song, Clarice became aware what real applause sounded like from the stage. It shook the stage as the old favourite of two generations, wearing her set smile, waddled back to the debutante. Scores of voices hoarsely shouted 'Encore!' and 'Last Rose of Summer,' and with a proud sigh the Lopez went on again, bowing.

Clarice saw nothing more of Otto, who doubtless had other birds to snare. The next day only three daily papers mentioned the concert at all. In fact, Otto expected press notices but once a week. All three papers praised the matchless Lopez in her Shadow Song. One referred to Clarice as talented; another called her well-intentioned; the third merely said that she had played. The short dream of artistic ascendancy lay in fragments around her. She was a sensible girl, and stamped those iridescent fragments into dust.

III

The *Staffordshire Signal* contained the following advertisement: 'Miss Clara Toft, solo pianist, of the Otto Autumn Concerts, London, will resume lessons on the 1st proximo at Liszt House, Turnhill. Terms on application.' At thirty Clarice married James Sillitoe, the pianoforte dealer in Market Square, Turnhill, and captious old Mrs. Toft formed part of the new household. At thirty-four Clarice possessed a little girl and two little boys, twins. Sillitoe was a money-maker, and she no longer gave lessons.

Happy? Perhaps not unhappy.

A LETTER HOME[2]

[2] Written in 1893.

I

Rain was falling—it had fallen steadily through the night—but the sky showed promise of fairer weather. As the first streaks of dawn appeared, the wind died away, and the young leaves on the trees were almost silent. The birds were insistently clamorous, vociferating times without number that it was a healthy spring morning and good to be alive.

A little, bedraggled crowd stood before the park gates, awaiting the hour named on the notice board when they would be admitted to such lodging and shelter as iron seats and overspreading branches might afford. A weary, patient-eyed, dogged crowd—a dozen men, a boy of thirteen, and a couple of women, both past middle age—which had been gathering slowly since five o'clock. The boy appeared to be the least uncomfortable. His feet were bare, but he had slept well in an area in Grosvenor Place, and was not very damp yet. The women had nodded on many doorsteps, and were soaked. They stood apart from the men, who seemed unconscious of their existence. The men were exactly such as one would have expected to find there—beery and restless as to the eyes, quaintly shod, and with nondescript greenish clothes which for the most part bore traces of the yoke of the sandwich board. Only one amongst them was different.

He was young, and his cap, and manner of wearing it, gave sign of the sea. His face showed the rough outlines of his history. Yet it was a transparently honest face, very pale, but still boyish and fresh enough to make one wonder by what rapid descent he had reached his present level. Perhaps the receding chin, the heavy, pouting lower lip, and the ceaselessly twitching mouth offered a key to the problem.

'Say, Darkey!' he said.

'Well?'

'How much longer?'

'Can't ye see the clock? It's staring ye in the face.'

'No. Something queer's come over my eyes.'

Darkey was a short, sturdy man, who kept his head down and his hands deep in his pockets. The raindrops clinging to the rim of an ancient hat fell every now and then into his gray beard, which presented a drowned appearance. He was a person of long and varied experiences; he knew that queer feeling in the eyes, and his heart softened.

'Come, lean against the pillar,' he said, 'if you don't want to tumble. Three of brandy's what you want. There's four minutes to wait yet.'

With body flattened to the masonry, legs apart, and head thrown back, Darkey's companion felt more secure, and his mercurial spirits began to revive. He took off his cap, and brushing back his light brown curly hair with the hand which held it, he looked down at Darkey through half-closed eyes, the play of his features divided between a smile and a yawn.

He had a lively sense of humour, and the irony of his situation was not lost on him. He took a grim, ferocious delight in calling up the might-have-beens and the 'fatuous ineffectual yesterdays' of life. There is a certain sardonic satisfaction to be gleaned from a frank recognition of the fact that you are the architect of your own misfortune. He felt that satisfaction, and laughed at Darkey, who was one of those who moan about 'ill-luck' and 'victims of circumstance.'

'No doubt,' he would say, 'you're a very deserving fellow, Darkey, who's been treated badly. I'm not.'

To have attained such wisdom at twenty-five is not to have lived altogether in vain.

A park-keeper presently arrived to unlock the gates, and the band of outcasts straggled indolently towards the nearest sheltered seats. Some went to sleep at once, in a sitting posture. Darkey produced a clay pipe, and, charging it with a few shreds of tobacco laboriously gathered from his waistcoat pocket, began to smoke. He was accustomed to this sort of thing, and with a pipe in his mouth could contrive to be moderately philosophical upon occasion. He looked curiously at his companion, who lay stretched at full length on another bench.

'I say, pal,' he remarked, 'I've known ye two days; ye've never told me yer name, and I don't ask ye to. But I see ye've not slep' in a park before.'

'You hit it, Darkey; but how?'

'Well, if the keeper catches ye lying down, he'll be on to ye. Lying down's not allowed.'

The man raised himself on his elbow.

'Really now,' he said; 'that's interesting. But I think I'll give the keeper the opportunity of moving me. Why, it's quite fine, the sun's coming out, and the sparrows are hopping round—cheeky little devils! I'm not sure that I don't feel jolly.'

'I wish I'd got the price of a pint about me,' sighed Darkey, and the other man dropped his head and appeared to sleep. Then Darkey dozed a little, and heard in his waking sleep the heavy, crunching tread of an approaching park-keeper; he started up to warn his companion, but thought better of it, and closed his eyes again.

'Now then, there,' the park-keeper shouted to the man with the sailor's cap, 'get up! This ain't a fourpenny doss, you know. No lying down.'

A rough shake accompanied the words, and the man sat up.

'All right, my friend.'

The keeper, who was a good-humoured man, passed on without further objurgation.

The face of the younger man had grown whiter.

'Look here, Darkey,' he said, 'I believe I'm done for.'

'Never say die.'

'No, just die without speaking.'

His head fell forward and his eyes closed.

'At any rate, this is better than some deaths I've seen,' he began again with a strange accession of liveliness. 'Darkey, did I tell you the story of the five Japanese girls?'

'What, in Suez Bay?' said Darkey, who had heard many sea-stories during the last two days, and recollected them but hazily.

'No, man. This was at Nagasaki. We were taking in a cargo of coal for Hong Kong. Hundreds of little Jap girls pass the coal from hand to hand over the ship's side in tiny baskets that hold about a plateful. In that way you can get three thousand tons aboard in two days.'

'Talking of platefuls reminds me of sausage and mash,' said Darkey.

'Don't interrupt. Well, five of these gay little dolls wanted to go to Hong Kong, and they arranged with the Chinese sailors to stow away; I believe their friends paid those cold-blooded fiends something to pass them down food on the voyage, and give them an airing at nights. We had a particularly lively trip, battened everything down tight, and scarcely uncovered till we got into port. Then I and another man found those five girls among the coal.'

'Dead, eh?'

'They'd simply torn themselves to pieces. Their bits of frock things were in strips, and they were scratched deep from top to toe. The Chinese had never troubled their heads about them at all, although they must have known it meant death. You may bet there was a row. The Japanese authorities make you search ship before sailing, now.'

'Well?'

'Well, I shan't die like that. That's all.'

He stretched himself out once more, and for ten minutes neither spoke. The park-keeper strolled up again.

'Get up, there!' he said shortly and gruffly.

'Up ye get, mate,' added Darkey, but the man on the bench did not stir. One look at his face sufficed to startle the keeper, and presently two policemen were wheeling an ambulance cart to the hospital. Darkey followed, gave such information as he could, and then went his own ways.

II

In the afternoon the patient regained full consciousness. His eyes wandered vacantly about the illimitable ward, with its rows of beds stretching away on either side of him. A woman with a white cap, a white apron, and white wristbands bent over him, and he felt something gratefully warm passing down his throat. For just one second he was happy. Then his memory returned, and the nurse saw that he was crying. When he caught the nurse's eye he ceased, and looked steadily at the distant ceiling.

'You're better?'

'Yes.'

He tried to speak boldly, decisively, nonchalantly. He was filled with a sense of physical shame, the shame which bodily helplessness always experiences in the presence of arrogant, patronizing health. He would have got up and walked briskly away if he could. He hated to be waited on, to be humoured, to be examined and theorized about. This woman would be wanting to feel his pulse. She should not; he would turn cantankerous. No doubt they had been saying to each other, 'And so young, too! How sad!' Confound them!

'Have you any friends that you would like to send for?'

'No, none.'

The girl—she was only a girl—looked at him, and there was that in her eye which overcame him.

'None at all?'

'Not that I want to see.'

'Are your parents alive?'

'My mother is, but she lives away in the Five Towns.'

'You've not seen her lately, perhaps?'

He did not reply, and the nurse spoke again, but her voice sounded indistinct and far off.

When he awoke it was night. At the other end of the ward was a long table covered with a white cloth, and on this table a lamp.

In the ring of light under the lamp was an open book, an inkstand and a pen. A nurse—not *his* nurse—was standing by the table, her fingers idly drumming the cloth, and near her a man in evening dress. Perhaps a doctor. They were conversing in low tones. In the middle of the ward was an open stove, and the restless flames were reflected in all the brass knobs of the bedsteads and in some shining metal balls which hung from an unlighted chandelier. His part of the ward was almost in darkness. A confused, subdued murmur of little coughs, breathings, rustlings, was continually audible, and sometimes it rose above the conversation at the table. He noticed all these things. He became conscious, too, of a strangely familiar smell. What was it? Ah, yes! Acetic acid; his mother used it for her rheumatics.

Suddenly, magically, a great longing came over him. He must see his mother, or his brothers, or his little sister—someone who knew him, someone who *belonged* to him. He could have cried out in his desire. This one thought consumed all his faculties. If his mother could but walk in just now through that doorway! If only old Spot even could amble up to him, tongue out and tail furiously wagging! He tried to sit up, and he could not move! Then despair settled on him, and weighed him down. He closed his eyes.

The doctor and the nurse came slowly up the ward, pausing here and there. They stopped before his bed, and he held his breath.

'Not roused up again, I suppose?'

'No.'

'H'm! He may flicker on for forty-eight hours. Not more.'

They went on, and with a sigh of relief he opened his eyes again. The doctor shook hands with the nurse, who returned to the table and sat down.

Death! The end of all this! Yes, it was coming. He felt it. His had been one of those wasted lives of which he used to read in books. How strange! Almost amusing! He was one of those sons who bring sorrow and shame into a family. Again, how strange! What a coincidence that he—just *he* and not the man in the next bed—should be one of those rare, legendary good-for-nothings who go recklessly to ruin. And yet, he was sure that he was not such a bad fellow after all. Only somehow he had been careless. Yes, careless; that was the word ... nothing worse.... As to death, he was indifferent. Remembering his father's death, he reflected that it was probably less disturbing to die one's self than to watch another pass.

He smelt the acetic acid once more, and his thoughts reverted to his mother. Poor mother! No, great mother! The grandeur of her life's struggle filled him with a sense of awe. Strange that until that moment he had never seen the heroic side of her humdrum, commonplace existence! He must write to her, now, at once, before it was too late. His letter would trouble her, add another wrinkle to her face, but he must write; she must know that he had been thinking of her.

'Nurse!' he cried out, in a thin, weak voice.

'Ssh!'

She was by his side directly, but not before he had lost consciousness again.

The following morning he managed with infinite labour to scrawl a few lines:

'DEAR MAMMA,

'You will be surprised but not glad to get this letter. I'm done for, and you will never see me again. I'm sorry for what I've done, and how I've treated you, but it's no use saying anything now. If Pater had only lived he might have kept me in order. But you were too kind, you know. You've had a hard struggle these last six years, and I hope Arthur and Dick will stand by you better than I did, now they are growing up. Give them my love, and kiss little Fannie for me.

'WILLIE.

'*Mrs. Hancock*——'

He got no further with the address.

III

By some turn of the wheel, Darkey gathered several shillings during the next day or two, and, feeling both elated and benevolent, he called one afternoon at the hospital, 'just to inquire like.' They told him the man was dead.

'By the way, he left a letter without an address. Mrs. Hancock—here it is.'

'That'll be his mother; he did tell me about her—lived at Knype, Staffordshire, he said. I'll see to it.'

They gave Darkey the letter.

'So his name's Hancock,' he soliloquized, when he got into the street. 'I knew a girl of that name—once. I'll go and have a pint of four-half.'

At nine o'clock that night Darkey was still consuming four-half, and relating certain adventures by sea which, he averred, had happened to himself. He was very drunk.

'Yes,' he said, 'and them five lil' gals was lying there without a stitch on 'em, dead as meat; 's 'true as I'm 'ere. I've seen a thing or two in my time, I can tell ye.'

'Talking about these Anarchists—' said a man who appeared anxious to change the subject.

'An—kists,' Darkey interrupted. 'I tell ye what I'd do with that muck.'

He stopped to light his pipe, looked in vain for a match, felt in his pockets, and pulled out a piece of paper—the letter.

'I tell you what I'd do. I'd—'

He slowly and meditatively tore the letter in two, dropped one piece on the floor, thrust the other into a convenient gas-jet, and applied it to the tobacco.

'I'd get 'em 'gether in a heap, and I'd—Damn this pipe!'

He picked up the other half of the letter, and relighted the pipe.

'After you, mate,' said a man sitting near, who was just biting the end from a cigar.

Also Published by the Echo Library By Arnold Bennett

NOVELS
Leonora
Sacred and Profane Love
Buried Alive
The Old Wives' Tale
Helen with the High Hand
Hilda Lessways
The Card
The Regent
The Price of Love
The Lion's Share
The Pretty Lady

FANTASIAS

The Grand Babylon Hotel

SHORT STORIES

Tales of the Five Towns
The Grim Smile of the Five Towns
The Matador of the Five Towns

BELLES-LETTRES

Over There
The Author's Craft (In Large Print)

Lightning Source UK Ltd.
Milton Keynes UK
21 June 2010

155902UK00002B/276/A